THE LYRICS TO HIS SONG

BY:

KRYSTAL ARMSTEAD

DEDICATION

This book is for my four beautiful children, Jada, Adrian, Jordan, and Angel. A life without you four is not worth living. This book is also for my beautiful step-children, Jamie, Jasmine, Anglie, and Little James. I love you all like you are my own. Never forget that.

ACKNOWLEDGEMENTS

Of course I have to thank my homie, Racquel Williams, for taking me underneath her wing. Without her, none of this would have been possible. This is my moment, and best believe, I'm gonna take it! Third contract and counting! You're stuck with me foreva (in my Cardi B voice)!

I also give thanks to Robin Watkins and Ashley Williams for keeping my spirits up when I want to give up. There are days when I don't want to get out of bed, when I'm just ready to give it all up and throw in the towel. But then, Robin curses me out, and I have no choice but to keep going! I appreciate ya, homie, for giving me that push that I need!

I can't forget about my homies in my reading group, Krystal's Motivation. Michelle Neal, Shanicia Jackson, Elysia McKnight, Octavia Carter, Glenda Daniel, Nicki Ervin, Kasey Smith, Monique Franklin, Fallon Hampton—these are my motivators! There have been days where I was too sick to get out of bed. One of them would message me on Facebook or text my phone, asking me, "Where the hell is my book, Krystal?" Even when I feel like giving up, even when I'm crying my eyes out over the daily stresses in my life, this crew always manages to put a smile on my face. I appreciate you all. There are too many to name, but just know I appreciate the love.

Thanks to my mother and father, Jennifer and Conrad Artis, Jr.

I'd like to thank my cousin, Latrese Washington, even though she has "deemed me uncousined" a few times! Muah! Love you, Cuz!

And last, but definitely not the least, my husband James. We stayed together through situations that were meant to rip us apart. The only way from here is up, boo. Let's go get this moneeyyyyyyy!

Thank you all for your support. Thank you God for the opportunity. A'ight, y'all, let's do this!

PROLOGUE

June 2016

Audrey "Lyric" Gibson

"Antwan, wait!" I called out to Antwan, as he strolled down the hallway with his entourage, on the way to the stage, at the Nokia Theater L.A. Live.

Antwan turned around when he saw me. He grinned, looking sexy as a muthafucka in his sky blue, button-down shirt, dark denim jeans, and high-tops from Roberto Cavalli's urban wear apparel line. His publicist liked my idea of toning him down a little bit. I wasn't trying to soften him up. I was just trying to get this man to cross over like Drake did. Appeal to a broader audience. If he wanted to be accepted by the mothers of these females that he was rapping to in his songs, he had to play the boy-next-door role sometimes. It was okay to show one or two tattoos every now and then. But this dude had tattoos that trailed from his hips all the way around his got-damn ear. His side burns were even tatted on.

It was Antwan's first appearance at the BET Awards, and though he pretended not to be, I knew this dude was nervous as hell. Shit, I was nervous. He was performing his first love song—a love song that I wrote for him. Antwan Jared was a gangsta rapper. Twenty-two-years old. Young, wild, and dangerous. He took the industry by storm when

1

he was just fourteen. Shit, producer Karen Black put the air under that troubled soul's wings, and he hadn't stopped soaring ever since.

"What's up, Lyric?" I loved when he called me that. He hadn't called me by my birth name, Audrey, since the day that he found out that I wrote music. Antwan smiled at me, chrome braces shining under the hallway's incandescent lights.

"You-you forgot your hat." I stuttered, handing him his sky blue 'The Hood Raised Me' baseball cap, the cap that his brother once wore.

"Awe, shit, thanks. You know I can't perform without my nigga." Antwan smiled, taking his hat from me, his fingers grazing against mine. I missed his touch. It had been a few months since he touched me, since I'd seen his face. My heart was in trouble from the moment I met Antwan Jared. In order to stay out of trouble, I tried my best to keep my distance. It wasn't easy, but it was for the best. A strictly-business relationship with that dude was damn near impossible.

I smiled up at him, about to wish him good luck, when a few of his dancers—my sister, Brandie, included, whisked by us, grazing against my shoulders on both sides. I glared at Brandie, knowing the bitch bumped into me on purpose.

"C'mon, babe." Brandie tugged on Antwan's arm. She slid her hands down his arms until her hands met his. She held his hand, pulling him away from me. She looked at the glare on my face and had the nerve to wink at me.

I rolled my eyes at my sister, looking her over from head to toe. There she was, wearing pretty much nothing. A white sky blue crop top, tiny dark denim shorts, and high tops. All the dancers matched Antwan's attire. I was dressed in a floral Dolche and Gabanna floor length dress, ready to take my place in the audience, in the first row.

Antwan slipped his hand from hers, adjusting his cap. He glanced at her and then looked back at me. "I want you on stage with me, Lyric."

I glanced at my sister, whose smirk was wiped clean from her face at that point. She loved rubbing the fact in my face that a guy like him would never be interested in a girl like me. That I'd never mean shit to a man who could have fifty of me on any given day of the week if he chose to. She said I had nothing he wanted but maybe the lyrics for his next song. She'd met the boy years before I did because she was that girl who did whatever she needed to do to get in any rapper's new video. I, on the other hand, was the manager of Foot Locker, who just happened to get lucky.

My boo, Mariah, scurried past me to catch up with the dancers. She was always late.

"Girl, you better hit that stage wit'cha nigga! This is it; fuck Sean!"

3

I looked back at Antwan as he held out his hand for me to take.

I looked at my sister and the rest of her dancers (also known to every rapper in the game as IP, or Industry Pussy). Rumors about Antwan and I had floated around for months. I tried keeping my distance from Antwan, but the more I tried to pull away, the more he tried to pull me back in. I wasn't supposed to be around him. I wasn't supposed to anywhere near him without Sean. That was the agreement that I made.

"C'mon, Lyric. We doing this shit together or what? I can't see myself doing this without you." Antwan watched me biting my lip nervously.

His team shook their heads at him.

"C'mon, Antwan, let's roll." His hype man, Drizzle, spoke up.

"Shorty doesn't wanna be in the spotlight; you know how she is. And her nigga, Sean, already told you that he doesn't want her on stage with you. He's out there now, standing behind that turntable on stage. What'cha think he's gonna do when he sees you with his girl? The nigga is gonna flip!"

Antwan ignored him, turning towards me. "Man, fuck that nigga. What I look like performing your song without you? I don't wanna do it without you. I won't do it without you, Ma." Antwan reached for my hand and grabbed it.

4

THE LYRICS TO HIS SONG

I gasped as he led me down the hallway with his crew.

The roar of the audience chanting his name echoed throughout the hallway.

"They stay ready for The Jeweler!" Drizzle was hype as usual. "Do what'cha want, bruh, but we both know the outcome. You already got enough beef with this nigga. You need to leave his girl alone. You've done enough damage."

My heart was pounding to the beat of the song, my song, as we strolled down the hallway towards the stage. "Sean is gonna be pissed when he sees me walking out on this stage with you, and you know it." I whispered to Antwan.

"Too muthafuckin' bad, shawty. You already know I don't give a fuck. You ready?" Antwan laughed a little, eyeing the nervous expression on my face as he led me down the hallway, intertwining his fingers with mine.

"No." I mumbled, looking up at him as I scurried along in my heels that I still hadn't gotten used to.

"Well, you better get ready. Cause it's show time." Antwan winked at me.

CHAPTER ONE

Face the Facts

"If I could mail my heart right to you, I would." I sang to myself, along with Zhane playing over the loud speakers at Foot Locker, one Friday morning, two days before Valentine's Day to be exact.

"I'd pack it up, seal it tight, and send it overnight!" My employee, and best friend, Mariah, came from the stockroom, twerking to the song, which was so not a song to twerk to. But then again, Mariah twerked to everything.

I shook my head at her, feeling a sharp pain in my chest. My chest always hurt when it rained, ever since that car accident that I was in four years ago. My family and I were visiting our relatives in Jacksonville, Florida, for Thanksgiving, 2012. My older brother, Alvin, and I were sent to get food from the grocery store. It had to be around seven in the morning when Grandma sent us out shopping for a few last minute items on her list. We were just laughing, joking, singing along to Dueces, my brother's fifteens beating down the block. We were stopped at a red light on that rainy day. When the light turned green, my brother took off, and we were hit by a man who fell asleep behind the wheel of an 18-wheeler. Alvin was killed instantly on impact. I, on the other hand, survived but just barely. I suffered severe blunt force trauma to my chest. My heart was damaged far beyond repair. I remember waking up in a hospital bed, camera lights flashing in my face, my parents standing at my side. Turns out, I was in a coma for three months. I had a broken collarbone, a fractured pelvic bone, and a broken left tibia. Why was I surrounded with cameras, news reporters, and shit? Because my life was saved by the mayor of Baltimore City, who was also vacationing in the area. Mayor Denise Jared-Michael was killed the same rainy day when her car hydroplaned off of the road, slamming her into a tree. She wasn't wearing a seat belt, and she flew through the windshield. She was an organ donor. She died and, because of her heart, I lived. Hundreds of people died each year waiting on transplants, and I was chosen.

"You okay, Audrey?" Mariah approached me, rubbing my back, watching me rubbing my chest.

I nodded. "Yeah, boo, I'm good. You know my chest hurts when it rains. Not to mention, my head is killing me."

Mariah shook her head at me. "Are you still having those nightmares?"

I looked at her. Ever since my heart transplant years earlier, I was having dreams about being raped and almost killed. I could never see the rapists face. But the dreams were too vivid to be dreams. They were almost like memories. But the memories weren't my own. I started doing research after the dream I had of giving birth to Antwan and Apollo. I found out that it had been scientifically proven that one-tenth of organ donor recipients took on the personality traits of their donors. And some even inherited their memories. I couldn't tell you how many times I intended on going to work at Arundel Mills Mall but ended up parked outside of the mayor's office to go to work.

I sighed. "Yeah, girl. I don't wanna talk about that shit right now though. Let's talk about you, hun. What'cha getting into tonight?"

"You mean, what are we getting into tonight?" Mariah grinned, her bright brown eyes widening with excitement.

"Fuck you mean?" I scoffed. "I have to open in the morning. I'm not trying to get drunk with y'all fools tonight. Besides, Sean is supposed to be taking me out tonight." I watched Mariah roll her eyes. "He's finally home. They're about to be gone on tour for another two months or so. I hadn't seen that boy for damn near three months, okay?"

My boyfriend, Sean Lee, aka DJ Sean, deejayed and produced music for rapper Antwan "The Jeweler" Jared. In case you didn't know, Antwan Jared was killing it in the rap game. He was one of the last real gangsta rappers there was. He rapped reality raps. He didn't just rap the shit; the dude lived it. And if his last name was familiar to you, that was because his mother was Mayor Denise Jared-Michael, the woman whose heart beat in my chest. I met Antwan once, but he showed no interest in meeting me. It almost seemed at the time that he resented me because I lived, the woman who he often rapped about losing died, and I lived on because of her. Sean took me to meet

Antwan one night, about three years ago, after I'd had my final heart surgery. Antwan barely looked at me, partly due to the fact that he was drunk and high as hell, with a groupie or two sitting on his lap.

"Girl, fuck that nigga." Mariah rolled her eyes. "That nigga ain't shit. The fuck you think he's doing out there while he's out on tour? Do you know how many times your sista rolls up in here, bragging, telling me and Elle about the freaky shit she does with those niggas and about the shit they do with other females? All those niggas in Sean's crew are dogs, going around humpin' every got-damn thing. You know your sister is IP, so she ought'a know."

I sighed. Brandie was a story all of her own. She was the result of a one-night stand with a Puerto Rican that my father had in between breakups with my mother. We were never really friends, though our parents made sure that we grew up knowing each other. We went to the same school for a few years and hung in different crowds. School was the last thing on this girl's mind. She skipped school every chance she got. She failed her grade at least twice. She was a grade ahead of me, so the only class that we had together was Spanish. And the only time she talked to me in class was to tell me to move my arm so she could copy off of my paper. How the fuck was this bitch supposed to be of Latin decent, but still managed to fail Spanish?

Underachievement at its finest.

KRYSTAL ARMSTEAD

Brandie had talent beyond words. Could dance more gracefully than any ballerina I'd ever seen. Instead of going to Julliard like she could have been, her ass decided that she was going to be a video vixen. She fucked her way through the industry to become a background dancer. She'd been in just about every rapper's videos, and just about every rapper had been in her. She was twenty-four years old and one of the most beautiful girls I knew. She was always competing with me, but I didn't see why.

I was a fuckin' twenty-one-year-old manager at Foot Locker. I was the responsible one, always told by my father to look out for Brandie as if she were the youngest. I was tired of being the responsible one. I wanted to wild out like she did every now and then but was too shy to do so. I wanted to write music; I was told that I was gifted vocally, but I was too shy to do that too. And Mariah was always trying to get me to test my skills on the mic at this club we'd visit in downtown Baltimore called The Rhymes. The Rhymes was like the hood version of Star Search. Every performance was televised on a local television station. Hundreds of careers took off because of that club. Producers, record executives, choreographers and celebrities from all over the country would visit that club every weekend, looking for talent. The club was run by some pretty ruthless muthafuckas who didn't play. The club owners were members of a squad known as the Royals. Their signature color was purple.

I laughed a little. " 'IP'? Don't you mean, IEP, Instinctive Entertainment Property?"

"Nah, bish, I meant just what the fuck I said. IP, Industry Pussy." Mariah rolled her big, pretty eyes.

I grinned at Mariah. My boo wanted to dance, too, and she was one of the baddest dancers around too. Her only problem was that she wouldn't dare do what the other girls did to make a name for themselves in the industry. I couldn't tell you how many auditions my boo made it through. She'd be so excited that she was chosen among thousands. Once she got through the auditions, and finally made it onto the set of a music video, that was when the shit hit the fan. After they would shoot a video, the rap stars would throw a party in whichever hotel they were kickin' it in. They'd have all the girls get naked. As soon as the word strip came out the rapper's mouths, Mariah's ass was flying out the door.

"You wanna dance too, huh, boo?" I made a pouty face at my girl.

Mariah rolled her eyes before her eyes started to coat over in tears.

"No… maybe… yes. Girl, stop playin', you know I wanna dance! But I wanna dance, not fuck niggas. Do you have any idea of the shit that goes on at those hotels?"

"Hell nah." I shook my head, rubbing my chest where it hurt as I sat down on the stool, behind the register.

"Well, I do. Those niggas make those girls take it in every hole by every nigga in their crew. And them dumb-ass bitches, your sista included, do that shit too." Mariah shook her head, face grimacing. "I ain't even trying to go out like that. I'ma make it someday. Last month, I auditioned for Anastasia Jones. She's always looking for new talent. Maybe she'll chose a sista, ya know?"

I grinned. "Of course she will, boo. She'd be crazy not to."

I was rooting for my boo. No one wanted the spotlight more than she did.

Mariah grinned back, nudging me in my side. "Like I asked, what'cha getting into tonight? A few of my cousins want me to roll with 'em to the club. You know Antwan Jared's making an appearance at The Rhymes tonight. I'm surprised Sean didn't tell you."

I looked at Mariah. Sean never told me anything. Sean liked to keep me out of his life when it came to the music industry. I had known Sean ever since I learned to tie my shoes. We'd been off and on since we were in junior high school. Sean was my first everything. First kiss. First touch. First taste. First dick. First love. And also the first boy to break my heart. He'd been mixing beats since that boy laid his hands on a keyboard in the second grade. When his older brother, Johnny, bought him that turntable and synthesizer in the seventh grade, oh it was on. You couldn't keep Sean off of either one of them. Sean started making mix-tapes. It didn't take long for his brother and cousins to realize that Sean had talent, that he could make money off of those tapes in the streets. The year before my car accident, a producer bought one of Sean's tapes. I'd never forget; we were chillin' at Popeye's off of 175 in Hanover when this man, who looked vaguely familiar, sat across from us. Turned out that familiar face was Rocky Moses, executive of Guttah Records, based out of Washington, D.C. He worked with a lot of local artists, but he was just big enough to get Sean where he needed to be. Six months later, my boo landed a spot on Antwan "The Jeweler" Jared's team, Instinctive Entertainment. And Sean hadn't been the same since.

Parties after parties. Tour after tour. Club after club. Bitches calling my house and hanging up at all hours of the night. Night sessions in the studio until around five or six in the morning, and you know that I was never allowed to go. I was stuck like glue to that boy. We'd broken up too many times to remember. And I took him back even more times than that. I couldn't say he didn't love me; but I couldn't say that his eyes, hands, lips, and dick didn't wander from time to time either. Yeah, I'd be the first to admit that I was dumb. Most of the girls that I knew who were dating celebrities at least lived with the muthafucka or he had her spoiled with all the material shit in the world that she was too busy being spoiled to realize that the nigga wasn't ever around. I, on the other hand, still worked at Foot Locker. Still struggled to pay bills. And still suffered from a broken heart. You see, when I'd gotten into that car accident back in 2012, I was three-months pregnant. I'd lost his baby. Can you imagine, waking up from a coma after three months to find out the baby inside of you was gone? I was devastated, and Sean was too busy making music to be hurt by the situation. As a matter-of-fact, Mariah told me that Sean had only came to see me once the entire time that I was in the hospital recovering.

"The nigga doesn't want you having a life, Audrey. There's no way you should be working here when your got-damn boyfriend, who you've known since you were a got-damn baby, is a fuckin' superstar! The nigga has headphones, drum sets, shit, got-damn cell phones named after him! His name, Sean Lee, is about to be every got-damn where, and where are you?" Mariah scoffed. "Working at Arundel Mills Mall in whack ass Hanover, Maryland."

I sighed, not really feeling like hearing her making sense that afternoon. "Girl, I ain't trying to hear this shit today. The new Jordan's came in this morning. You wanted a size five and a half in boy's, right?" I watched a smile form across my bish's face.

She threw her arms around me. "Girl, why you gotta be so sweet? Ugh! He doesn't deserve you. You're too good for him. Let's get fly, push these C-cups up, and twerk our way into The Rhymes tonight." Mariah watched me roll my eyes.

Before I could respond back to her, my bestie and assistant manager, Elle, came racing through the entrance, screaming.

"The fuck is wrong with you?" Mariah watched Elle jumping up and down at the counter, titties bouncing up and down. She wore a tight tank top, baggy gray sweats, and fresh gray Jordan's. Elle was Filipino and cute as a button but loud and ghetto as hell.

"Girllll, ooooohhhh! You will never believe who is about to roll up in here in about twenty seconds!" Elle screamed, just as a crew of four or five men dressed in all black made their way through the entrance of my store. They looked like someone's bodyguards.

Before I could even ask what the hell was going on, in came about six other men, dressed in white and purple urban apparel. They grinned at the three of us staring at them as they walked through the store. And just when I thought why the fuck did these guys need bodyguards, in strolled sexy ass Antwan Jared. Mariah's mouth dropped open. She damn near passed out at the sight of the dude; she had to brace herself up against me.

I shook my head to myself, standing up from the stool, eyes trailing Antwan as he made his way over to us. He was dressed in black Nike Sweats, a white tank top, black and white Jordan's, and a black baseball cap that read 'The Hood Raised Me'. I tried not to stare, but I found myself reading each and every one of the tattoos that decorated his shoulders, biceps, triceps, neck, and sideburns. He was sexy, in a you-don't-need-to-be-drooling-over-this-guy-because-you-have-a-crazy-ass-boyfriend kind of way. I wasn't quite as star struck as my girls were. My sister was a dancer, and my boyfriend produced music for superstars. I wasn't quite a part of their world, but I was affected by it. I was left out of so much of what was going on with either of their lives that I saw no fascination in it. My life hadn't changed one bit since either of them entered into fame. I resented fame. And at that moment, I pretty much resented Antwan. I bet the muthafucka didn't even recognize me or realize who I was. Not only was I the recipient of his mother's heart, but I was girlfriend of a man who produced the majority of his music.

I watched as the bodyguards, without my got-damn permission, let down the gates to the entrance of my store. Then, I looked back at Antwan's little entourage as they walked along the walls, looking at our selection.

Antwan looked at the three of us.

By that time, Elle was behind me, squealing under her breath. And Mariah was on the stool that I once sat on, grabbing onto my arm, digging her nails into my wrist. I sighed, shaking my head at Antwan, who chuckled at their thirst.

"Good morning, Mr. Jared, can we help you?" I watched as at least twenty people stood outside of the gate of Foot Locker, peeping in at Antwan. It didn't take but a few seconds for the crowd to realize who he was and start going crazy. I looked back at Antwan, who was grinning, platinum braces entrapping his teeth. This guy was the only dude I knew who could make braces look cool.

And I rolled my eyes. "It would have been nice if you would have had your agent or your manager warn us about you coming here. It's 10:00 on a Friday morning, the Friday morning before Valentine's Day to be exact. Most college students are out of school today. We make a lot of money the last few days before holidays, hun, so closing the store down while you and your little friends walk around, looking at shit really isn't making me any money."

Elle gasped.

Mariah looked up at me like I had lost my mind.

And Antwan grinned, shaking his head at me. I think the guy was pretty amazed that I wasn't falling all over him. There Mariah and Elle were, motionless, speechless, breathless over this dude. And all I could see when I saw Antwan was a troubled soul. All he rapped about was madness, murder, and mayhem, something that was foreign to me, the child of two middle-class parents who were from Florida.

Antwan looked down at the nametag on my shirt and then back up into my face. "Audrey, hey, what's up? How are you? Can me and my crew check out'cha shoes? We're hittin' up the club tonight. Not tryin' to roll up in there with my Giuseppe's when nigga's in Baltimore be with that bullshit. All we wanna do is buy about three or four pair of shoes each. There's twelve of us, so that's forty-eight pair of shoes.

17

Most of your Nikes and Jordan's run about $160, with them new J's being about $250. So, we're at least gonna spend a good," Antwan counted in his head for a few seconds, "$7700 within the next thirty minutes or so. When is the last time this store made that much in less than an hour, shawty?"

I sighed, nodding, agreeing with his reasoning. "Ladies, could you help these men find whatever size for whatever shoe they're interested in?"

Elle and Mariah were enjoying their time talking and trippin' with Antwan's crew. I was just chillin' behind the counter, trying to ignore the phone, which was ringing off the hook. I already knew that my neighboring stores were calling to complain about the crowd that was forming outside of my store, taking business away from them.

Antwan's song, Pop it for a G, played over the stereo system. I giggled to myself, watching Mariah bend over and twerk for the crew. You know them niggas were lovin' watching Mariah work her hips and clap that booty. She was just having fun, but all men think about when they see ass is getting in that ass. Little did they know, dick was the furthest thing from Mariah's mind. I'd known Mariah since second grade, and she'd always liked girls. There was nothing about a man that Mariah found appealing. The day that Mariah's father left her mother on her deathbed was the day that Mariah swore off men altogether. Her mother was dying, and the worse part was her father was sleeping with the oncologist that was treating his wife. Mariah watched her mother die of cancer alone. And a few months after her mother's funeral, her father moved the doctor into his home. From that day on out, Mariah was like, the hell with men. I saw her reasoning. Men be with that bullshit… but the dick is just so good. And if I wanted to play with pussy, I'd play with my own. I was just sayin'.

"So, you gonna give us a discount or what?" I heard Antwan's raspy voice coming from my left. I looked up to see Antwan strolling over to me, placing two boxes of Nikes and two boxes of Jordan's on the countertop.

I watched as Antwan pulled the price tag from the white shirt with black swooshes sprinkled over it that he held in his hands. I watched him pull it over his head, sliding his arms through the long sleeves.

I laughed to myself, watching Antwan put his baseball cap back on his head, adjusting it to his liking. "Ummm, and what do you call yourself doing?"

"Trying on the shirt that you're about to buy for me. Ya know, as my apology gift." Antwan grinned.

"Apology gift? Apologize for what?" I looked his flawless face over.

"For not saying a word to me the whole time I've been in this store. I know you've seen a nigga staring at you." Antwan's light brown eyes searched my face.

"I'm sorry. I was just distracted by the two hundred people standing outside of my store, waiting to get in to not buy shoes but to get your autograph." I rolled my eyes, trying my best to ignore his flirtation. "Mall security has called several times. I hope y'all plan on paying mall management for this commotion. They only welcome superstars when they get their cut, too."

Antwan looked at me for a minute, squinting his eyes as if to get a closer look at me.

"Wait, I know you, don't I?" Antwan tried remembering where he'd seen me.

I just looked at him. At the time that I was introduced to him, Antwan was going through a lot. The media had just exposed the fact that his mother was the Mayor of Baltimore, who practically disowned the man and his twin brother. Rumor had it, his father, who he'd never met, showed up to the funeral. His father turned out to be A.J. Miller, founder of Relentless Entertainment, a record label known for taking what they wanted by any means necessary. The company stayed in competition with Instinctive, often stealing artists from the company. Antwan and his twin brother, Apollo, were raised in public housing, in a community called Meade Village. Two boys who were supposed to be rich grew up in the hood, a place they had no business being. Antwan was angry, and it reflected in his music.

Antwan still remembered my face, and it surprised me. When I met him three years earlier, he was high as a kite and barely looked at me. Sean didn't have the heart to tell him that I carried his mother's heart around with me, but his manager thought him knowing that his mother was still alive and beating inside of someone would help Antwan's situation. It didn't. Antwan couldn't even look me in the face. That was the only time that Sean had ever brought me around his circle of people, and even then, I don't even think he introduced me as his girlfriend.

"No, we don't know each other." I shook my head, entering my manager ID into the register before scanning Antwan's shoes into the system. I didn't want him associating me with my sister, who danced for him, or Sean, who produced half the songs on his album. Brandie swore up and down that Antwan Jared was feelin' her. I didn't care what Antwan rapped about, every female thought his song had something to do with her. Whenever you'd see Antwan rapping on stage, Brandie was right there, front and center of the dancers. On Antwan's videos, there Brandie was, all over him. I didn't know what was going on, but I knew I didn't want any part of it.

"You sure? You look real familiar. I never forget a face. Especially not a face like yours." Antwan's eyes searched my face as he pulled out his wallet, taking out his American Express Black Card.

I shook my head, changing the subject. "No charge." I slid his shoes into two plastic bags.

Antwan looked at me, watching me sliding the shoes over to him. "What'cha mean, shawty? Your manager is gonna fire your ass."

"I am the manager, sweetie." I tightened the strings on the bags, holding them up so he can grab the strings. "Take 'em. They're my 'apology gifts', remember? And you can have the shirt, too, since you just threw it on like the shit was yours."

Antwan chuckled, taking the bags from me, his fingers grazing against mine. "That's what's up, Audrey." Antwan looked back at his people, who were still picking out shoes and flirting with my girls, and then he looked back at me. "Aye, what'cha getting into tonight? You got plans?"

I nodded. "You can say that. My boyfriend is just coming back in town after being gone for a while. We're gonna spend some much needed quality time together tonight."

Antwan's eyebrows lowered. He actually looked disappointed that I had a man, but he shook his feelings off real quick. "What'cha doin' workin' when your man needs to be takin' care of you, Audrey? Some nigga you've got." Antwan shook his head. "Sorry muthafucka."

I sighed, thinking the same thing myself.

"So, this is what you do? Manage shoes and shit?" Antwan grinned, braces sparkling.

I watched him lick his lips, and then I looked back into his eyes.

"Ummm," I stuttered, speechless for a few seconds. His lips were so fuckin' juicy. "I write music. I mean, not professionally, but I play around with a few lyrics every now and then." I entered my discount into the system before taking my debit card from my pocket to pay for the shoes.

Antwan watched me paying for his shoes. "So," he hesitated for a few seconds, probably stunned that someone was buying him something for once. "You're beautiful, work at Foot Locker, have a man, you write music, and you don't mind spoiling ya nigga. Do you ever do anything with your skills?"

"What do you mean?" My eyes searched his face.

"Just what I said, shawty. Do you ever put your skills to the test?" Antwan's eyes searched my face, too.

I hesitated. "Not often. My girls are always trying to get me to spit rhymes on stage. I do every once in a while, when I'm drunk, just for fun."

Antwan nodded. "That's what's up, Lyric."

I looked up at him. He had me from the word 'beautiful' but giving me a nickname really struck my heart. "Lyric?" I whispered.

Antwan grinned, "We're gonna be at The Rhymes tonight around 9:30. You know, the spot that my brutha and cousin manage downtown. My man, Trap, just gave ya girl three tickets to get in. Everything is on us. The drinks, the food, the transportation, everything. I'll even have my driver come scoop you and your girls in my ride."

I shook my head. Sean wasn't having that shit.

Antwan sighed, frustrated a little. "Or, if you don't want me to know where you stay, you can come on your own. C'mon, why don't you roll through? Spend some time with ya nigga in V.I.P. Afterwards, we're going over my man's crib for the after party."

I hesitated, looking over at my girls, who were looking back at me talking to Antwan. I looked back into his face.

Antwan still tried to convince me to go. "I'm sure you heard about the talent contest tonight. Whoever wins will get an interview with Karen Black, the CEO of my squad, shawty. You could earn a chance to work with my team. You just said that you write music. That you have skills. I bet you're pretty good, Lyric. Show me what'cha got."

THE LYRICS TO HIS SONG

I sighed as the receipt printed for his shoes. I tore the receipt from the feeder and then handed him the receipt. "If you have any issues with these shoes, let me know, okay? I'm here at least six days a week. If I'm not here, my assistant manager, Elle, is here."

Antwan smiled. "You are cute as a muthafucka." He watched me blush, something I didn't do too often. "And you've got the prettiest brown eyes I've ever seen. Does your man tell you how pretty you are?"

I looked up at Antwan, shaking my head, being honest with him. "He's too busy to tell me much of anything these days. I appreciate the compliment, Antwan, but I'm sure you tell all the girls they're pretty. Don't scuff the new Jordan's, okay? I'm sure we'll be sold out of size tens by tonight."

Antwan grinned, shaking his head at me.

"Aye, Jeweler!" One of Antwan's crew members, who I recognized from one of his videos, called out to him. "We're good. I think we have enough shoes. Let's pay shawty and roll, so we can hit the streets. We gotta get the rest of the crew from the airport."

"A'ight, Rhandy." Antwan answered him, looking at me.

"That accent of yours is sexy as a muthafucka. Bet you would have the crowd hype as a muthafucka. Just think about it."

I looked at him, watching him looking me over a little before turning around and walking away from the counter and over to his crew. Alright, heart, calm down, wrong person, I tried telling myself.

***

I sat at my dining room table that night, tapping my fingernails against the cherry wood surface. There it was, around eight that night, and I still hadn't seen Sean's ass. We were supposed to meet at six that night so that we could go out to eat and then to a movie. Sean hadn't so much as called me once that evening to explain why he was late. I sat there, looking cute, curly hair braided into a curly Mohawk. I was dressed in my white crop top, tight, high-waist jeans, and the knee-high, gray Jordan boots that Sean had custom-made for me a few months earlier. They were one of the many I'm-sorry-for-fuckin'-up-again presents. I loved that muthafucka with everything I had, but a person wasn't going to keep being dumb forever. I was tired of being kept out of his life. I was tired of being placed in the background. I knew at least five girls who were dating celebrities, and every last one of them went to at least two of their man's award ceremonies. They had at least been on tour with their man once. They had at least met their man's boss. They had at least been in one photo in one magazine with their man. My man had been working with Antwan Jared for five years, and I'd only met the crew once. And even that was only because Karen Black wanted Antwan to see that his mother's heart was still beating. But even then, I was only introduced as the recipient of his

26

mother's heart and not as Sean's girlfriend. Sean and I were getting nowhere.

I rolled my eyes as I heard Sean's key's jiggling outside of the door to my townhouse. I lived in a quiet neighborhood in Pasadena. For the most part, I spent most of my time there alone. Sometimes, my girls, Mariah, Elle, and Fatima, who dated one of Antwan Jared's drummers, would spend the night at my place to keep me company. I had a white and blue Pit named Steel to keep me company when my girls weren't around. He'd fuck your ass up if you even raised your voice at me. He was one of Sean's apology gifts. And I think that dog loved me more than Sean did. He lay asleep at the foot of my bed. That dog used to love Sean. Over the years, he'd gotten used to Sean not being around. He used to race to the door as soon as he heard Sean's car pull up outside. Now, all he did was grunt when he heard Sean's keys jiggling at the door.

"Where have you been?" I huffed, turning around to face Sean as he strolled through the front door, wheeling his brown Gucci suitcases behind him.

That nigga was fine as fuck. Every time I saw his face or even felt his presence, my stomach did back flips. I swear, you put this nigga next to R&B artist August Alsina and you couldn't tell the difference. And the worst part about him was that the nigga knew he was fine. He knew he was talented. He knew he had too many hoes chasing after him to let one hoe, me, get on his got damn nerves about where he'd been and what the fuck he was doing with his time. It didn't help that the muthafucka had a dick the size of his forearm either. This nigga was the definition of 'cocky'.

"What's good, shawty?" Sean took a deep breath, parking his suitcases behind my sofa.

I stood from the table, facing him, arms folded. "You forgot that we had plans, Sean?" I watched him stroll over to me, dressed in all white and purple, from his hat to his Guiseppe high-tops.

Sean walked over to me, looking my hair over. He smiled, perfect white teeth gleaming. Why did he have to be so damn fine? "Damn, you look good as a muthafucka, shawty. All this for me?" He grabbed me to him, unfolding my arms.

I looked up into his face. "Fatima called me, said your flight landed at two o'clock today."

Sean looked down into my face as he removed his hat from his head.

I looked over his neatly trimmed mustache and the finely trimmed hair on his chin. I looked back into his eyes.

"Fatima needs to mind her own got damn business. She needs to concentrate on little drummer boy and stop worrying about what the fuck I do. Yeah, my flight landed at two o'clock. I've been at the studio with The Jeweler and his crew since about 3:30. Afterwards, we went out for drinks." Sean slid his cool hands around my bare waist.

He knew his touch drove me wild, which was why the muthafucka always touched me when I was mad at him. Just one touch, one look from that boy, always set my soul into flames. I hated how much I loved him because I'd forgive him for just about anything he'd done. The muthafucka was lying to me. I don't think Antwan even finished signing autographs at my store that day until around 5:30. After security got rid of the crowd, I had to lead Antwan and his crew through what us mall employees called The Tunnel, which was the hidden inside tunnel entrance behind the outlets. Antwan and his crew walked as slowly as they could, along with me and my girls, trying to make sure that we were going to hit up The Rhymes that night. Antwan said he was signing me up to perform because he wanted to see what I was working with. I told him that I'd try to make it but that I wasn't making any promises. When Rhandy told Mariah that Serene, Joy, and Roxanne from the dance group, Black Beauty, from Howard University were going to make an appearance at the club that night, you already know she was on it. The word was out that this group was working closely with Anastasia Jones. Elle just wanted to be a part of the mix, so she promised to go with Mariah. I think Antwan talked to me in the back of the mall until around 6:30 that night. So, wherever Sean was, it wasn't with Antwan.

"You're lying." I looked into his face, watching his nostrils begin to flare. He hated when I questioned him. He hated when I got all "insecure" on him. "I don't know where you were, but it sure as hell wasn't with Antwan and his crew. You're always standing me up, Sean." I pushed his hands off of me. "I haven't seen you in months, and the first place you'd rather be when you step foot in Maryland is not with your girl? The girl you've known since elementary school? My birthday is Sunday, got damn Valentine's Day; do we have plans or not?"

Sean's eyes just searched my face. I hated that 'I could really give a fuck what you're talking about' look that he always wore on his face. Sometimes, that nigga cared, and sometimes, he didn't, and that shit always drove me crazy.

"Are we supposed to have plans?" Sean watched my eyes grow bigger before I rolled them. "I have mad work to do all weekend, Ma."

"Ugh!" I screamed out in frustration, walking past him. "Sean! It's fucked up enough that I have never been out with you or your boys, but now you're in town after being gone three months, and you're about to be in the studio with them on my muthafuckin' birthday? Can I go to the studio with you? Shit, we can have dinner there."

Sean laughed to himself, following behind me. "Nah, Audrey. You don't wanna be around my niggas. The spot is gonna be filled with purple haze, liquor bottles, and groupies. Oh, and IP might roll through too. They practice there in the studio."

I stopped in my tracks, turning around to face him. "Oh, so my sista can hang with you, but I can't be there with you?" I was hurt.

Sean's face grimaced. "What? Audrey, it's not the environment that I want my sweet girl to be a part of. I'ma be mixing beats all got damn weekend. As a matter-of-fact, I gotta be there tonight at 9:00. I just came here to drop my bags off."

I was pissed. I shoved Sean in his chest with both hands.

"You are so got damn selfish! You don't give a fuck about me! I've been sitting here, waiting on you, and the first thing you do when you get home is work? I'm sick of this! Get'cha shit and get out!" I pushed past him, on my way to his luggage that he parked by my couch.

Sean found my anger hilarious. "Bae, why you trippin'? Why you mad, huh? Why are you always in ya got-damn feelings?" He grabbed my hand, pulling me back to him before I grabbed his shit. I was about to sling that shit outside in the yard. "You want me to beat the pussy up, huh? That's why you mad?"

"I want you to stay with me tonight, Sean! We don't have to go out; I just want a little bit of your time. You don't have time for me! I've known you damn near all my life, and all I get out of you are texts, tags on Facebook, and maybe five-minute phone conversations!" I looked into his face, trying to pull from him, but Sean grabbed my face, kissing my lips. I melted in his mouth as he kissed, nipped, and sucked on my lips. I moaned in his mouth. Kisses were a rarity with that nigga, so when I got a kiss from him, I embraced the moment, never knowing when or if I'd receive another one. "Sean, I miss you. Please stay with me tonight!" I squealed as Sean started to unsnap and then unzip my jeans.

"I wanna stay with you, bae, but I've got work to do tonight. I won't be out late; I promise." Sean whispered between kisses, unbuckling his belt, unsnapping and then unzipping his jeans. "Turn that ass around."

I shook my head, eyes growing misty. "Sean, a quickie? That's all you've got for me?" I panted as Sean started to push my pants over my hips.

Sean quickly turned my body around. "Grab the couch," he whispered in my ear before kissing my neck, right behind my ear. That was one of my spots, and he knew that shit too.

The only time we were in tune was when it came to sex. Any other time, we were just on two completely different pages; shit, we were in two completely different books, in completely different genres. I didn't even know how we'd lasted so long.

I grabbed the couch as Sean quickly pulled that long, thick, dick of his out of his pants. I braced myself, gasping as Sean wrapped his arm around my waist, pressing his body up against mine, holding my body close. He didn't bother to play with the pussy to get her wet because he already knew that as soon as he asked me if I wanted him to beat the pussy, she was already drooling. Like I said, I wished I didn't love him so much. But he was all I knew. He was my first. I gave myself to him for the first time while he was dating someone else back in high school. It was prom night. I went to the prom with some other dude and still ended up in Sean's bed that night.

Sean panted in my ear as he eased his way inside of me. My pussy collapsed around his penis, sucking it in, gripping it tight.

"Got damn, there's no place like home." Sean laughed in my ear, arm wrapped around me, hand gripping my hip.

"Stay with me tonight, Sean…" I sighed as he began to stroke. I couldn't tell you how many years it took to get used to Sean's dick. He was the only man I'd ever been with sexually, and any man after him would have a lot to live up to when it came to sex. Sean wasn't the least bit romantic, but his stroke was on point. If he held me after sex, if he would slow down a little and let me enjoy the moment, he would be just right. We never once made love. The only way Sean could ever make me cum was when he ate me out. Not saying I didn't love to feel his lips on me, but I always had to reciprocate. His dick was humungous, and my gag reflex was real serious, y'all. The sex was amazing, but we never connected on a spiritual level. I never felt at one with him. He was always so distant. The only time we had sex missionary was on prom night, four years ago. I needed a connection with Sean, not a quickie. It was as if he was afraid to connect with me on any level. The only time this fool needed me was when he wanted me to help him write music, which he never gave me credit for.

I think Sean might have gotten four pumps in when his iPhone rang in his pocket. The nigga didn't stop pumping, but he slowed down a little and actually answered his phone.

"Really?" I panted, looking back at him.

"What's up?" Sean spoke through the phone.

I couldn't hear the conversation but I could hear the muffled sound of a woman's voice.

"A'ight, I'm on my way," Sean said before ending the conversation and putting the phone back in his pocket.

I whimpered a little as he pulled out of me. "Seriously?" I looked over my shoulder at him, watching him pull his pants up, zip them, and then buckle his belt. I turned around, facing him, pulling my panties up, then my pants. "I'm not even worth a quickie? Who the fuck was that?"

"Karen Black. She needs me to roll with her to the studio." Sean watched the irritated expression on my face. "Don't look at me like that. She's the entire reason for my existence in the music industry. When she calls, I haul ass."

I looked into his face as I buttoned my pants over my waist. I folded my arms, watching Sean dig through a pocket on his suitcase. He pulled out a royal blue velvet box. I already knew what it was before he turned to me with the box and opened it. It was the diamond, platinum cuff bracelet that my sister wore on her wrist. I guess Sean thought I didn't notice. He must have forgotten that I had a sister who bragged about the jewelry that she was laced with. She claimed that the CEO of IE gave all of the dancers the same bracelet, though she was the only one who I saw with it on. But if Sean wanted me to play dumb, I was going to play dumb.

I looked at Sean as he looked down at my wrist, sliding the bracelet onto it.

"I gotta go." Sean kissed my left cheek before turning around, walking away from me.

"Sean!" I called out to him. "What time are you coming home? Are you coming home?"

Sean grinned at me over his shoulder, putting his purple cap back on his head. "No matter what I do or who I'm with, don't I always come home?"

And then he left me. Alone. As usual.

CHAPTER TWO

You and that Bitch

"I can't believe that I let you two talk me into this." I sighed, nervous out of my mind as me, Elle, Mariah, and Fatima stepped out of Fatima's red Porsche that night in the parking lot in front of The Rhymes.

"Well, believe it, girl." Fatima rolled her big brown eyes as she stood alongside me, dressed in her burgundy fitted silk dress and black Red Bottoms. She was dressed to kill. As were the rest of my team.

"That nigga is in this club, Audrey. I'm telling you; my bae said he's in this bitch. Said he's in here with your got damn sister. I say you slip your ass backstage and surprise this nigga with your skills, right in front of that bitch."

I shook my head to myself as Mariah slipped her arm around my waist.

I looked at my girl.

Mariah looked at me, sympathizing with my pain; at the same time, revenge was written all over her face. "That nigga pulled out'cha pussy to come here so he could get up in hers tonight. I'm telling you, he's fuckin' your sister. Get in here, rock this mic, and get this job. You don't belong at Foot Locker. Sean has been using your lyrics against you for years. That's your shit he's been rewriting, making the shit hood. He's good, but you're better. And you need to show that muthafucka tonight. Now let's go."

I was sweating bullets as my girls trailed in front of me, down the red carpet, straight into the club that night. The place was packed. I'd been there a few times with my girls, but it was never that packed. Antwan was in town; that was what it was. He almost never came to his brother's club. I didn't know much about Antwan, but what I did know was that he used to be a member of the Royals. He still rocked purple every now and then to let the world know he was Royal until he died, but he didn't do the dirt for them that he once did. His twin brother, Apollo, was knee deep in the shit. Apollo was the leader of the Royals. As much as Antwan hated the life, I was sure he hated to see that his brother was never letting go.

"There he is." Elle whispered in my ear as we made it to the end of the hallway entrance to the club. She pointed over at Sean, who was hand and hand with not only Brandie but with her friend, Cara, who was a dancer as well.

I shook my head as Fatima grabbed my hand. "That muthafucka."

"Girl, fuck that nigga. Come on, girl." Fatima rolled her eyes.

"I got us the table right in front of the stage. Y'all grab a seat, and I'll meet y'all there. I can't wait to see the look on that nigga's face when Audrey kills this shit!"

THE LYRICS TO HIS SONG

Fatima had more confidence in me than I had in myself. I was hurt when I saw Sean with my sister. I already knew the nigga wasn't working that night, but to tell me that he was working and then I saw for myself that he was with Brandie… Yeah, I was ready to show out that night. I didn't feel much like singing or flowing. Reciting my poetry and singing to myself in the shower or at work in between customers was one thing, but to perform on stage in front of Karen Black or Antwan Jared was another thing. I was so ready to just forget the whole thing, go out there on the floor, and beat the fuck out of my sister in front of Sean, until I saw Antwan backstage, talking to everyone who was about to perform that night. He was so down to earth and so friendly, nothing like the celebrities that came to that club who were too much to even shake your hand or give you an autograph. He shook the male performers hands and hugged the ladies. One of the contestants was even crying when he hugged her. He dried her cheeks and kissed her forehead. And then he saw me, walking backstage, still dressed in my high-waisted jeans, knee-high Jordan's, and white crop top.

"You came. That's what's up." Antwan's braces sparkled as he smiled at me, watching me and Fatima walk up to him that night backstage. He looked me over. "That's a cute outfit. Sexy but comfortable. Looks like something a girl made for me would wear."

I blushed, looking down at my feet.

"Can't wait until you take the stage tonight, shawty. I'm geeked like a muthafucka that you showed up." Antwan told me.

I sighed, looking him over a little. That nigga was too fine. My eyes traced the tattoos that trailed up his neck and around his ear. I looked back into his face. I stood there, holding my leather notebook against my chest. I must have written over three hundred songs in that book. It was my lyrical journal. I wrote in it every day. I hadn't shared it with anyone, but that day, I was about to share the song that I wrote about Sean on the way over to the club.

"My girl here is the best you've ever heard, Antwan." Fatima put her arm over my shoulder, laying her face against mine, her straight hair brushing against my face. "Aye, contestants, listen up: my chick here is about to win this contest. No offense to any of y'all, but y'all might as well just go the fuck home."

Antwan and I both looked at her crazy ass, shaking our heads.

Fatima rolled her eyes. "Antwan, you've been around me enough to know that I hold no punches. See you out there on the dance floor, Audrey!" Fatima kissed my cheeks, and strolled her way from behind the purple curtain.

Antwan shook his head at me. "I had no idea you were friends with Fatima's crazy ass. She dates my nigga, Snare, my drummer."

I nodded. "Yeah, me and Fatima go way back to fifth grade. She used to date my brother."

"Oh yeah? Well, what happened to that relationship? He couldn't handle all that crazy, huh?" Antwan grinned.

I exhaled deeply. "No. He died four years ago in a car crash."

Antwan's grin faded. "Car crash? Awe, man, shawty, I'm sorry." He looked down at the scar on my chest, over my heart. Then, he looked into my face. "Were you in that car crash too?"

I nodded, forgetting that I was actually wearing something that showed a little cleavage for a change. Although I wasn't ashamed of my scar, I didn't want anyone asking about it. It only reminded me of losing my brother.

"Yeah. The only reason I'm alive is—"

"Are y'all ready?" I was interrupted by the infamous Karen Black.

Antwan still looked at me, like he was trying to figure out where he knew me from. I think it was starting to come back to the boy when he saw that scar of my chest.

I turned my attention to Karen Black as she strolled through the ten of us that stood backstage, ready to show our skills to the rowdy crowd behind those curtains. Karen looked like the chocolate version of Sade. She was tall with the prettiest, deep bronze-colored skin. Her long hair flowed down her back, trailing down her beige Gucci dress.

She had to be at least 5'10" without those heels. She was once a model, but once she married old school rapper, Ervin Black, she started producing music and was great at it. Everyone on her label had made it double platinum. Her crew stayed in the media's eye. Tour after tour. Concert after concert. Acting gig after acting gig. Collaborations. Book deals. Magazine spreads. Radio interviews. Clothing lines. Restaurants. Endorsements. Rumor had it that the company was going bankrupt, but I didn't see how. Instinctive Entertainment was everywhere you turned.

Karen caught sight of me with Antwan, and she winked at me, grinning, deep dimples stinging her left cheek. "Okay, ladies and gentlemen, I'm looking for a few good song writers. I only need three. I picked the three cities that I'm choosing from. That's here in B-More, then I'm headed to Miami, and then to Houston. I'm short on time, so this performance tonight is going to make or break you. I'm only choosing one of you to interview tonight after the show. No pressure." She laughed, watching the nervous expressions on all of our faces.

"My husband, the executive producer of IE, is going to be out there watching. Not to mention myself, Antwan the Jeweler, and our hot DJ," Karen glanced at me, "Sean Lee. Sean Lee is the reason why we're in need of new song writers."

I looked at Karen.

"He is about to leave me for a few weeks and go work for Relentless." Karen announced something that I had absolutely no idea about.

My eyes widened. "Wait, what?"

Antwan looked at me, eyebrows lowering a little, probably wondering why Sean was of any interest to me.

"Okay, lyricists," Karen clapped her hands together. "Showtime in three minutes. Audrey?"

"Yes?" My heart sank in my chest.

"You're up first. Kill this shit. The press is watchin'." Karen winked her eye at me before turning around, leaving backstage, making her way front stage. You should have heard the screams coming from the crowd. "Hey, how y'all beautiful people doing tonight?" Karen's voice filtered the room, followed by whoots and squeals.

I took a few deep breaths, trying to pace my breathing and control my heart rate.

"So, yo, how do you know Karen?" Antwan faced me, adjusting my crop top a little, fingers gracing against my torso as he pulled my shirt down a little. He looked me over before looking into my face. "Sean Lee? That's your nigga?"

I just looked at Antwan, heart rate speeding up, as Karen told the audience about the talent show I was about to perform in first.

"So, you're not gonna answer me, huh, Lyric?" Antwan shook his head at me, looking down at the bracelet on my wrist. He looked back into my face. "Did the nigga give you that bracelet too? I'm asking because my dancer, Brandie, has the same bracelet on tonight."

I sighed, rolling my eyes. "Brandie? Yeah, that's my sister." Might as well tell him; he was bound to find out sooner or later.

Antwan's eyes widened a little before shaking his head at the situation. "Well, the nigga just gave your sister a new pair of earrings. Not to mention, what looks like a big ass hickey on the side of shawty's neck. Seems to me like he's her man."

I frowned, all nervousness subsiding.

"You should've fallen for someone who deserves your heart instead of falling for someone who was just gonna play with the muthafucka." Antwan whispered to me.

I looked at Antwan. "That's what niggas are good at; playing games, and trickin' us into falling in love with y'all when y'all know y'all ain't ready."

"Not all of us, shawty." Antwan shook his head in disagreement.

"Sean doesn't represent us all. Some of us are too old to play games. You need to tell that silly muthafucka that tricks are for kids."

I nodded. "Oh, I intend to, when I get out there on stage."

"A'ight, let's see then." Antwan dared me.

"Audrey Gibson?" Rip, the co-owner of the club, stepped backstage.

I looked up at him as he walked towards us.

Rip walked up to Antwan, giving him some dap before looking me over. "You're up, Ma. Rip that shit."

I looked at Antwan, who was grinning at me, looking me over too.

I sighed, rolling my eyes, leaving the two of them standing there.

"Good luck!" The other contestants rooted for me as I left backstage, making my way front stage. Boom, there everyone was, surrounding the stage, all eyes on me. It was a lot to take in. I looked down at the people surrounding the stage, and then I looked out at the tables seated around the room.

"Audrey! Whoot!" My girls were cheering me on at the table to the left.

I laughed nervously, eyes searching the room until I saw Sean's ass sitting at a table in the center of the club with my sister, her friends, and a few of his boys. You should have seen the look on Sean's face when he saw me standing there on stage, standing there in front of the microphone.

"How is everyone doing tonight?" I spoke up after a few seconds of my stare down with Sean. Oh, he looked just as pissed to see me as I was to see him. As pissed as I was, it felt so good finally showing the skills that Sean was scared to unleash. And the look on my sister's face was priceless. I didn't know whether the girl was shocked that the sister she claimed didn't have the balls to get in front of a crowd was actually standing on stage in a room full of hundreds of people. Or if she was scared of what I was going to say after seeing the two of them together when they claimed they despised one another.

I grinned a little, as the crowd cheered me on, as the band behind me started to play a slow groove. I adjusted the microphone stand, hands trembling a little, as my nervousness began setting in again. "Ya know, a lot of y'all know me from the Foot Locker at Arundel Mills. Yeah, that's me, the one y'all stay tryin' to get to hook y'all up with a discount. A few of you know that I write music. I'm a writer, not a rapper or a singer, so bear with me. My girls talked me into doing this bullshit."

My girls whistled. The crowd laughed, all except for hating-ass Brandie and shaky ass Sean. The more I looked at those two together, the more courage I got to face them both.

"This song is dedicated to all the niggas who fucked us over because we let them." I sighed through the microphone, getting hundreds of amens from the crowd. "This song is dedicated to all the niggas who keep on playing games, whose lovin' ain't the same, like they just know we're here to stay. Like a bitch not gone get tired of his shit." I removed the microphone from its stand, my eyes focused on Sean and then on my sista. "This song is also for the bitches who can't keep their muthafuckin' hands off our men. Who can't find a man of her own. Who fucks her way to the top. Who thinks she's playing you but she's playing herself." I held my middle finger up high, towards my sister and Sean. The crowd cheered me on. "Fuck y'all. I call this song... Sean Lee Doesn't Belong to Me..."

Oh, all eyes were on Sean, the nigga who was ashamed to let the world know that he was dating an average-looking brown-skinned girl. I was good enough for him as long as nobody knew what I looked like. Brandie was industry pretty, sitting there looking like a mix between Alicia Keys, Paula Patton, and Jhene Aiko. Ya know how it is. Us black chicks were cool until the nigga thought he'd come up. Not realizing that the black woman in his life was the only reason why he even got the chance to meet those girls.

The beat of the drums resonated throughout my body. The saxophone player had my soul feeling so good. Queen Gates hummed into the microphone to my far left. She was a bad vocalist who refused to leave the club. She didn't want any label trying to own her. In the club, she could do her own thing. She knew how the industry worked. She knew it would change her into someone that she didn't want to be.

Queen Gates always played by her own rules. I looked at her over my shoulder as she winked her eye.

I exhaled before I opened my lips to rap my lyrics.

"Are you ready to talk now? Seems like you're always too busy for me; after all that we've been through, I can't get a minute. Wow. I don't ask for much; maybe a kiss, maybe just a touch. Maybe you can hold me once in a while; there used to be a time when you'd do anything to make me smile. I remember when you'd stroke my insides until my legs went numb; do you remember me screaming in your ear, 'I'm about to cum, nigga, I'm about to cum!'" I laughed.

The crowd hollered.

Sean slouched back in his seat.

Queen Gates hummed behind me.

"I lived you, I breathed you, I loved you, nigga, I needed you." I sang, tears forming in my eyes.

"You know I needed you." Queen ad-libbed.

"I told myself that I wasn't gonna write another song about a nigga who could give two fucks about me but... you pulled out of me to pull into her. You said you loved me, you said you'd never leave me, so why the fuck are you sitting here with her? I'm tired of the lying, I'm tired of the crying, I'm tired of loving you when I'm the only one who's trying..." I rapped to Sean.

48

"You ain't shit, nigga. Time to pack your shit, nigga…" Queen sang, neck roll, eye roll, and all.

The crowd cheered us on.

Brandie rolled her eyes, glancing at the expression on Sean's face.

I exhaled before I sang, "I'm not worth your time; no one knows you're mine. You're ashamed of me, was blind but now I see. I was there when you needed me, but you won't give your heart to me. Now I see why you can't love me, too busy lovin' my sister, Brandie. Slangin' wood, up to no good; the kind of love I needed, you never understood." I started rapping again.

"You'd never understand that all I wanted was for you to be a man. My man, nigga, not hers, not theirs; you were supposed to be mine, Sean, why the fuck do I have to share?"

"I needed love, nigga." Queen whispered through the mic.

"If her bed is where you lay your head, come get your shit, you and that bitch." I hissed through the mic, the crowd cheering me on. "I wasted so much time trying to make your heart mine." I whispered. "You never belonged to me because that bitch is where you always wanted to be. So, let's end it right here, let's just end it at that; once you walk out that door, there's no coming back. Enjoy your life, don't come looking for me; once it's over, it's over, you're gonna miss me,

Sean Lee…" And I dropped the mic, walking backstage, as the crowd chanted. I walked past Antwan, who was trying his best not to grin.

I made my song short, sweet, and to the got damn point. I really had no interest in winning the contest. I just wanted to show Sean that I was no fool. That I knew he was fuckin' around with my sister. That I knew he lied to me about where he was going that night. I loved that fool, and all he loved was himself. Too in love with his own talent to realize I had talent too. He kept me in a box, never wanting me to break loose. I needed a little polishing, but the talent was in me. And after that night, he couldn't deny it. Shit, I was the one who helped him stay up all night writing music. Music that I wasn't getting paid for writing. It wasn't Brandie's ass who helped him into stardom. It was me, got damn it. I didn't want to win the talent contest; I just wanted to beat my sister's brains in, in front of Sean. I had to get out of there before I went to jail. I was tired of people taking my non-ratchetness for a weakness. I'd fuck a bitch up over mine, only… Sean wasn't even mine. He made that known when he showed up to the club with that bitch.

I tried to sneak past the other contestants and dart out the back door. I don't think I made it five feet from the back entrance when I heard Antwan calling my name.

"Aye, where you goin', Lyric?" I heard footsteps behind me.

I looked back to see Antwan standing at the foot of the stairs. I sighed as Antwan walked up to me. It was cold as hell outside, and there I was, trying to be cute in a crop-top.

Antwan shook his head, watching me standing before him, shivering. He took off his jacket, throwing it over my shoulders.

"Where the fuck is your coat?"

"I-I left it in the car. You know muthafuckas at your brother's club be stealin'." I rolled my eyes, watching Antwan smiling down at me.

"Where you goin', Ma? Why you leaving me so soon?" Antwan asked, licking his lips.

I shook my head. "I just wanted to see for myself that the nigga was here. I didn't really plan on winning. I just rapped and sang a song to y'all that took me five minutes to write, that I wrote in the car on the way here."

"So," Antwan made a face. "You didn't come here for me; you came here for him? To prove something to that nigga?"

I sighed. "Antwan, honey, I don't know a got-damn thing about you. All I know is what I see on television, and what I see on television is a boy who's too scared to be a man. You rap about a life that you should have outgrown by now. Your lyrics are full of anger, full of pain, full of fear. You live on the edge. You're hood than a muthafucka, Antwan, when you should be straight-Hollywood. You still hang with all the niggas you used to fuck with in Meade Village. You're rockin' all this purple shit, like you're one of the Royals, even though you claim not to be affiliated with them. You talk all that shit in your songs, yet as I stand here face-to-face with you, I don't see any of that shit you spit in your music. I see a scared little boy who wished he knew his mama."

Antwan's eyebrows knitted together, his eyes searching my face. "I thought you just said that you didn't know a 'got damn thing' about me."

I just looked up into his face.

"You got the job." Antwan huffed, shaking his head at me.

"What?" I asked, watching him walk back up the stairs leading to the club.

He tapped on the door, looking back at me standing there in his jacket. "You had the job when I saw you swipe that card to pay for my shoes, shawty. You showed love, so I gotta show it back."

I shook my head, walking back up the steps to the club, taking his expensive jacket from my shoulders, handing it back to him. "You know that's not fair, Antwan. Those other contestants are talented! You need to give them a chance."

Antwan nodded. "A'ight, let's let the crowd choose."

And the crowd chose me that night. I won by popular demand, not by Antwan's vote alone. My girls were happier than a muthafucka, but I was nervous out of my mind. And you already know Sean was mad as hell, looking at me like he wanted to ring my neck for revealing that I was the girl that he was hiding from everyone. Karen Black invited me to VIP to sit and chat with her that night. I told her I would if I could bring my girls with me. Of course she agreed, especially since she already knew Fatima. I tried to slip past Sean, but he grabbed me by my wrist, pulling me to him, my sister and her friend, Lola, at his side.

I glared at my sister a little before looking back at Sean.

"What the fuck are you doin' here?" Sean growled.

"What the fuck are you doin' here? With this bitch at that?" I pulled from him.

"You don't know what you're getting yourself into, Audrey. Take ya ass back home." Sean demanded. "You don't need to get involved in this shit. Go the fuck home, Audrey!"

"Listen to your man, sis," Brandie grinned, nudging Sean.

Oh, you know I wanted to beat the hoe shit out of Brandie, but I didn't. I let it ride. Why? Because she needed the attention more than I did. Even though I wanted to walk away, Mariah wouldn't let me.

"Ya know, the last time I saw you, you had dick in your mouth." Mariah pushed me to the side and got in Brandie's grill.

"Here, let me give you something else to put in your mouth." And Mariah punched the bitch right in her mouth.

There my best friend was, trying to rip that girl's face apart, and there I was, breaking up a fight, and there Lola was, trying to jump in to defend my sister. Sean backed away as security rushed over to break us all apart. Of course, Mariah was thrown out of the club. I tried to go with her, but she shouted at me that I needed to stay, that I needed to sign the dotted line on the contract we knew I was about to be presented with. Fatima and Elle took Mariah home after telling me that they'd see me at the after party. And I watched Sean carry my sister out of the club to Lola's car so she could get her to the hospital. Watching him with her broke my heart all to pieces.

There I sat in VIP, watching all these record executives poppin' champagne. Just that morning, I was working at Foot Locker, doing inventory. But there I was that night, sitting amongst some of the biggest record executives in the country. And I should have been excited, but I wasn't. My life was about to change, and I wasn't sure which direction it was about to go. I sat there in a booth, across from Karen Black and her husband, Ervin. I took a deep breath as Antwan slid into the booth next to me. I slid over a little to give Antwan his space, but he slid next to me, as close as he could get.

I sighed, rolling my eyes, glancing at him and then looking at Karen Black as she slid the contract across the table to me. I took the contract in my hands, reading it over, not understanding shit that I read.

"Congratulations, Audrey Gibson, and welcome to Instinctive Entertainment." Karen smiled, her pearly white teeth gleaming under the lights.

"Don't congratulate me yet; I haven't signed anything." I put the paper down. "I'll have to get a lawyer to look this over."

Karen laughed a little, looking my face over. "Seriously?" She glanced at Antwan who slouched back in the booth next to me. She looked back at me, nodding. "Okay. The contract looks a little intimidating, yes, I know, but look at the figures. When have you seen that many zeros? Everyone thinks it's the artist who makes all the money, but no, honey, it's the people that are behind the scenes that get all the bread. The label pays you, the artist pays you, the radio stations pay you, the television stations pay you—I'm telling you, you will never see bands like this, honey! Tell her, Antwan."

"Well, if I'm gonna be making so much money, why is Sean leaving your company?" I had to ask.

Ervin spoke up before his wife could explain it to me. "Your boyfriend—ya know, the boyfriend who didn't tell anyone that he even had a girlfriend—isn't leaving us. Until this merge is over, he's going to go work with Relentless Records for a few months."

Antwan made a face, sitting up in his seat. "Whoa, wait, what merge? Merge with who?"

Karen sighed, as if she was tired of always arguing with those two. "Antwan, honey, listen before you start poppin' off."

"I don't wanna listen to shit if it has anything with going into business with A.J. Miller!" Antwan started going off.

"Nigga, he's your father." Ervin shook his head in disgust at Antwan.

"The father I didn't even know I had until my mother died four muthafuckin' years ago. Did y'all even ask me what I thought about this bullshit before you decided to make a move like this? Do y'all know what goes on behind the walls of that muthafuckin' tall ass building he works in? Ervin, you ain't even about that life, bruh." Antwan shook his head as the server in VIP brought more champagne bottles over to our table.

"Well, what if I am?" Ervin huffed.

Antwan laughed out loud. "Nigga, your shit is Will Smith, and his shit is Eazy-E, straight-outta, Compton type shit. Nigga, trust me, you ain't ready. Karen, you better tell 'em. Didn't you use to fuck with that nigga back in the day?"

Ervin glanced at Karen and then back at Antwan. "Slow your roll, Antwan, don't get disrespectful."

Antwan shook his head. "You ain't seen disrespectful. You do business with A.J. Miller and I guarantee you it won't be your bed Karen is sleepin' in, it'll be that nigga's."

Ervin was about to jump across the table on Antwan, but Karen grabbed her husband back.

"Look, fellas, chill! Antwan, this merge is good for our company. The only heavy hitter we have on our team as far as rappers are concerned is you; Relentless Records has everyone. They have Chopper, A.J. 47, DJ Paper, Roulette, and Blade. I've been trying to sign Queen Gates forever, but she won't budge. We need a vocalist, someone who can sing, rap, and write music." Karen glanced at me and then back at Antwan. "By merging with them, we'll have their entire fan base as well as yours."

"Yeah, and y'all muthafuckas will have their problems, too." Antwan shook his head at the two record executives. "Yo, maybe it wasn't a good idea to bring shawty here tonight. I don't want her involved with this shit. The smartest thing Sean ever did was keep her out of this bullshit. But luckily, Karen, I spoke with your lawyer who helped me revise your contract a little."

Karen looked at Antwan. "Revise my contract a little? What do you mean? Let me look this contract over. I knew I couldn't trust

Michael." Karen reached for the contract, but Antwan put his hand over it, making sure it stayed put, right in front of me.

"I made a few revisions that your boy, Sean, is gonna love, shawty." Antwan grinned, braces gleaming.

It's funny he mentioned Sean because, as soon as he mentioned Sean, Sean came strolling into VIP, looking pissed. Our eyes met, and once they did, Sean was making his way over to me. He got to the table, eyeing all four of us, before he locked stares with Antwan.

"Let's go, Audrey," Sean said to me, though he was looking at Antwan.

Before I could even respond, Ervin speaks up.

"So, Sean, this is the girlfriend you never told us about." Ervin smirked. "You never told anyone you had a girlfriend, that y'all have known each other your whole life, that y'all have been dating off and on since junior high. How come we've never met this beautiful, talented young lady?"

Sean's nostrils were flaring. "Nigga, I introduced her to y'all three years ago. Karen wanted Antwan to meet the girl who had his mother's heart. Remember?"

I sighed, feeling Antwan's eyes searching my face. He was probably trying to figure out why the hell I was trying to play him when he knew that he knew me from somewhere.

"Yeah, bruh, your mother's death is the reason why Audrey's still alive. The entire reason why she's sitting here beside you. The entire reason why I'm taking the girl back home. The entire reason why she's not working with you, nigga." Sean snarled.

I looked up at Antwan, who still looked me over a little, before he frowned up at Sean.

"'The girl'? We know she's yours and you're still not claiming her? If you care about 'the girl' so much, why the fuck is she here tonight? She didn't even come here to audition; she came here to catch your ass with her sister. She came here to prove a point to your ass, nigga."

Sean glared at Antwan as Antwan stood from the table, stepping out of the booth.

"And what point is that, nigga?" Sean snarled up at Antwan.

"That she doesn't belong to your ass because you never claimed her, muthafucka. Don't come in here, telling shawty what the fuck she's not gonna do when you weren't worried about what she was doing when you were out there doing what you were doing." Antwan looked Sean in the face.

Ervin stood from the table, signaling security to make their way over to our booth.

Sean looked Antwan over like Antwan had him fucked-up.

"Nigga, this the game you wanna play?"

"What game is that, Mr. Deejay?" Antwan laughed at Sean as if he were joking.

"You get in the way of me and Audrey if you want to, nigga, and you'll see. This ain't the life for her, homie. I didn't want her having any parts of this shit. You gonna protect her from the bullshit we deal with every day, muthafucka? Nigga, you can't even protect your got damn self!" Sean pushed Antwan in his chest.

Security made their way over, about to grab Sean, when Antwan signaled them that it was cool, that he had the situation under control.

"Nigga, when I thought you were going to work with A.J. Miller, turns out, you're taking songs written for me to his artists. You all have no idea what type of ruthless muthafucka my father is, nigga. You don't wanna involve your girl in this shit, nigga, when she's already involved. You're making a mistake by involving yourself with this nigga; you all are. When that nigga bleeds y'all dry, don't come lookin' for me. And as for Audrey—" Antwan looked down at me and then back at Sean. "Nah, bruh, Audrey stays here, with me."

Sean frowned at Antwan and then looked at me as I stood from my seat, making my way out of the booth. I had to get a better look at Sean. I looked him over a little, eying the lipstick smudge on his neck, right above the collar of his shirt. I shook my head to myself before sliding the diamond bracelet from my wrist, grabbing his hand, and placing the bracelet in it.

"You should go check on your girl, Sean, see how her face is doing." I whispered, just when Sean yanked me to him my forearm, squeezing my arm as tightly as he could.

I yelped as he yanked my body to his.

"Bitch!" he yelled when security pulled him up off me and damn near had to drag him out of the club. "Antwan, you touch her, you're dead, nigga! Do you hear me? Fuck with her if you want to, muthafucka, and see what happens! Audrey, I'll see you at home."

My heart pounded in my chest. I'd never seen Sean that upset. He never cared about anything. He damn sure didn't care about me once he got his taste of fame. I didn't know why he was causing such a scene over a girl whose sister he was fuckin' around with, in front of everyone, knowing it would eventually get back to me.

I looked at Antwan as I rubbed my forearm.

"Audrey, you don't need to go home. He didn't sound like he was playin'." Karen tried to tell me. "He's been drinking all night and—"

I laughed it off, looking over at Karen. "Karen, it's cool."

"I can send security with you." Karen watched me laughing.

"Karen, nah, I'm good. I've known Sean all my life. I'm not scared of that fool. He's just upset when he really has no right to be. As a matter-of-fact, hand me that contract." I turned to the table as Karen gave the contract to me again.

"Well, apparently, I'm guessing the revisions that Antwan made to your contract include you working directly for him. Is that right, Jeweler?" Karen rolled her eyes over from me to Antwan.

I looked at Antwan.

Antwan grinned. "Got damn right."

I sighed, watching him bite his lip.

"So, he's your boss. You report directly to him. We'll go over the rest of the paperwork tomorrow. Yes, we work weekends. Bright and early. Meet me in my office at 7:15 sharp." Karen let me know, watching me grab the pen from the table and sign my name on the contract without even reading it over. "I know you're the manager at Foot Locker and all, but that shit needs to take a backseat. Better yet, leave that shit at the curb and pull the fuck off."

I held the signed contract in my hands, thinking about my boo, Mariah, who didn't have anyone in her life who believed in her the way that I did. "Before I give this to y'all, I need to ask a favor."

Karen nodded, looking at her husband and then back at me. "Sure."

"See, there's this dancer I know, my girl, Mariah—" I started off.

Ervin laughed out loud. "That girl who just tried to knock my dancer's face off?"

I nodded, watching the couple shake their heads at me. "Yes, my best friend, the chick I grew up with. I'm asking you to let her audition for your dance crew. As a matter-of-fact, I want y'all to sign her. She's brilliant. She's a hell of a lot sexier than the hoes you have on your dance team now, my own sister included. No her, no me, simple as that."

Karen grinned. "You drive a hard bargain, but I like it. I think we made the right move with this one. Okay, honey, you've got a deal. Welcome to Instinctive." Karen held out her hand to shake mine.

"Yo, Lyric, hold up!" Antwan called out to me that night as I walked to my car.

I looked over my shoulder at him before turning around to face him in front of my black Dodge Challenger.

Antwan grinned, looking over my clean ride. He looked me over before looking in my face, the smile clearing from his face. And he cleared his throat. "So, why didn't you tell me you knew me after I told your ass that you looked familiar?"

I shrugged.

"Don't give me that shoulder shrug shit, Lyric. You knew we met before. And you weren't gonna say shit." Antwan's eyes searched my face.

"Well, we didn't exact meet. I was introduced to you; you didn't even look up at me once you heard that I was the recipient of your mother's heart. You kinda just brushed me off and went back to partying with your crew." I watched Antwan exhale deeply. "You were pretty hurt. I guess you didn't wanna meet the person who survived because of your mother's death."

"Is it true?" Antwan asked.

"Is what true?" I asked back.

"What they say about organ donor recipients. They say you take on the personality, thoughts, and memories of the person who gave you their organs. My mother gave you her heart; what else did she give you, Ma?" Antwan asked.

I shook my head, not wanting to tell this boy the nightmares that I had just about every night about what his mother endured.

"Nightmares."

"Nightmares? About what?" Antwan's temples twitched a little.

I hesitated. "I don't know yet. But she went through some shit, Antwan."

Antwan shook his head at me. "Man, I had no idea that we were merging with A.J. Miller. That nigga is ruthless. I know you're only doing this to get back at Sean, but be careful. I'ma look out for you though."

I scoffed. "Look out for me? You need to be looking out for yourself, boo. I saw how those niggas were lookin' at you tonight at the club."

It was no secret that the Royals were always into it with their rival gang, Murk. These niggas didn't play any games. They would murder niggas in broad daylight, in front of crowds of people. No mask, nothing but Russian street artillery. Baltimore was their stomping ground, and they didn't appreciate the Royals, a smaller gang that originated out of a group of boys from Meade Village apartments, nvading their territory. Apollo was the leader of the Royals. He'd come a long way from being a poor kid on welfare. I didn't know much about Apollo or Antwan before the surgery, but once I met Antwan face-to-face, it was as if memories of the boys growing up invaded my mind. Antwan was right; I told him that I didn't know shit about him, but there I was, feeling like I'd known him forever. My heart beat stronger with every word that came out of Antwan's mouth.

Antwan scoffed. "Them niggas ain't gonna do shit. The Royals are a crew of very few, but trust me, there isn't always strength in numbers. Anyway, let's get back to what I was sayin' about you. Why didn't you tell me that you have my heart, I mean, my mother's heart? I knew there was something about you." Antwan watched me blushing a little. "And you're right. I never knew my mother… but I wanted to. And since you have her heart, I have no choice but to try and protect it."

I just looked up into his face, not really sure what to say except, "So, what makes Sean and the Blacks want to work with A.J. Miller?"

Antwan exhaled deeply, looking at me like he really didn't feel like talking about it. "The Blacks are in debt like a muthafucka. Not payin' muthafuckas and shit. Your nigga threatened to walk out, sign with A.J. Miller. I had no idea that they were merging companies. I guess Ervin thinks that A.J. can save 'em. I'm trying to tell him; he has no idea the kind of shit that he's about to have to do for this paper. A nigga is about to branch off on my own once my contract is up. This next album is about to be dope as fuck. I'm producing the majority of the album on my own, without ya nigga. And I have a production company in the works; you're the first artist that I'm signing. I hope you read the fine print on that contract. You work for me, remember that when Karen tries to run that 'you work for me and my husband' shit on you, a'ight?"

I sighed, apparently having no idea what shit I'd gotten myself into. "I just wanna write, Antwan," I admitted. "I don't wanna be involved with any bullshit. I already have to figure out how I'm gonna tell my boss that I quit without notice. I don't wanna leave on a bad note when they've done so much to help me. I mean, my boss, the area manager, Korey Phillips, pays my rent! He bought my car! Sean hasn't done shit for me but break my heart. I don't know how I'm gonna tell them."

Antwan grinned. "Invite them to lunch tomorrow. Fuck what Karen is talkin' about. Go to work. Do your inventory thang or whatever you do bright and early at your store. And then, meet me in time for song rehearsal around 11:00. A'ight? Invite your managers. And make sure that Mariah comes with you. Shit, fuck dancing—she can be your bodyguard!" Antwan acted like he was Mariah, throwing left and right hooks. "That girl can fuckin' fight!"

I laughed out loud. "Yeah, Antwan, she's my ride-and-fuck-em-up chick! I love her. I gotta take her with me. I'm all she has."

Antwan smiled. "And she's lucky to have you. Must be nice to have someone to depend on. Someone who keeps you outta trouble. The muthafuckas I roll with keep a nigga involved in some bullshit."

I just looked at Antwan as he adjusted the hat on his head.

"You comin' to the after party tonight?" Antwan asked me, eyes tracing my lips.

I shook my head. "Nah, I better get home."

"Get home to that nigga who you just said back in that club ain'tcha nigga?" Antwan grinned.

I rolled my eyes, not really feeling like explaining to someone who I'd just met the extent of how much Sean meant to me. I was pissed at Sean for everything he'd taken me through over the years, but before he walked out of my life, I needed an explanation. I already knew Sean was going to go straight to my place and pack his shit. He had walked out before. I should have let him go, but I'd let him walk right back in when he got tired of running the streets. Only for him to turn around and do the same shit over and over again. Why he continued to hurt me, I had no idea. I just wished he'd love me.

"I just wish he loved me, Antwan." I didn't mean to say that out loud.

"Why would you settle for a muthafucka like him when you could easily have a nigga like me?" Antwan told me.

I looked up at him. "You don't even know me."

"I know all I need to know. All I'm saying is you need to save that heart for someone who cares about it." Antwan shook his head, looking down at the contract that I held tightly in my hands. He looked back into my face, changing the subject. "My contact information is on the last page of the contract. Call me when you need me, Lyric."

THE LYRICS TO HIS SONG

I drove home that night to find Sean sitting in the living room, leaned back on the sofa, smoke floating in the air. I sighed, closing the front door behind me. There were no bags packed as I expected. In fact, the nigga was in a white t-shirt and black sweats, making himself completely at home. At home on a Friday. It was raining outside and this nigga had my poor Steel sitting on the back porch.

"What part of 'pack your shit, you and that bitch' don't you understand, Sean?" I strolled over to the coach where he sat, standing before him.

Sean looked at me, exhaling smoke from his mouth and nose, watching me fold my arms. "The part that doesn't explain how the fuck you figure that I'm fuckin' around with Brandie. The part that doesn't explain why the fuck you think it was cool to pop up at a club where muthafuckas get sprayed just about every other weekend. The part that explains why you think I'm about to let you work with Antwan Jared." Sean got up from the couch.

"Let me work with Antwan? Nigga, you don't own me!" I pushed him in his chest.

"What do you mean how do I figure you're fuckin' around with Brandie? Nigga, y'all were holding hands and the same shade of lipstick she wears was on your collar! You bought me the same bracelet that you bought her!" I shoved him again. "And I showed up to the club because that's exactly where you weren't supposed to be

69

tonight, since you said your ass was supposed to be in the studio with the crew! You didn't tell me that they were airing the talent show live! You didn't tell me that Instinctive Entertainment needed another songwriter. You didn't tell me that you were working for A.J. Miller or that the company was merging with his."

"Merging?" Sean made a face. "The nigga is taking over the shit. Ervin sold his company to A.J. Your boy will be glad to hear his father is about to own every right to every song that he's ever written. You don't wanna get in the middle of that family shit, shorty, I'm telling you. I've protected you from the shit all these years, and your dumb-ass wants to jump right into it because you think by working with this nigga you're hurting me."

"I'm tired of not meaning shit to you, Sean. I'm somebody. I'm fuckin' important. You might not think I am but—" I yelped when Sean snatched my forearm, pulling my body up against his.

"But what?" Sean snarled in my face. "He thinks you're important? You fuck around with that nigga and see what the fuck I do to your ass, Audrey."

I tried to pull from him, but he wouldn't let me go. That look in his eyes scared the hell out of me. He was drunk. Probably had been doing some of every type of drug that night. Who knows. All I knew was he wasn't exactly himself. We stayed arguing. Stayed waking up the neighbors when we argued. But one thing he'd never done was put his hands on me. That was going to change that night. Steel already started growling, pressing his face against the glass sliding door.

"Nigga, you ain't gonna do shit!" I finally yanked from him.

"You're fuckin' around with my sister and have the nerve to tell me who you don't want me to be around? Fuck you and that bitch!" I turned around to walk away from Sean when he yanked me back to him by my hair. I grabbed his hands, trying to pull them from my hair, but he was gripping the shit out of my hair.

"The next time you embarrass me out in public, in front of hundreds of muthafuckas, on got damn television, in front of reporters and shit, I will beat your muthafuckin' ass!" He gripped my hair in his hands, pulling my body up against his, his eyes tracing my profile, my hands gripping his wrist. "You got that shit?"

"Sean!" I squealed as this muthafucka pushed my body over the arm of the sofa, yanking my jeans and panties down over my hips. I screamed out, Sean still gripping my hair with all of his might. Steel started barking and howling outside of my door. As loud as he was barking, you would have thought the neighbors would have been banging on my door, but no one showed up to help me.

"You're mine. Do you get that shit, Audrey?" Sean growled.

"You belong to me. You let that nigga know that shit. I told you that I didn't wanna include you in this lifestyle. You never listen to me, Audrey. I bet you'll listen now, won't you?" I felt him pulling his pants down, his hard dick poking me in my butt cheek.

I cried out. "Sean, no! What are you doing?" I felt him search for the opening to my butt with his dick. And as soon as he found it, he shoved all eleven inches of his dick through my rectum, into my body. My legs damn near gave out from under me. It hurt so bad that I couldn't even scream at first. My body tensed for a few seconds before I could even let out a shriek or make any sound at that. "Sean, stop!" I screamed.

"You wanna feel how these niggas do these bitches in this industry? A'ight. I'll show your hard-headed ass." Sean let go of my hair and gripped my neck instead. With his free hand, he pressed my back down, my stomach digging into the arm of the chair. He didn't ease his way through me; he forced his way through me. Through the ridges and over the hump until he found the perfect fit. He started to stroke, despite my screams and efforts to get him off of me. I started kicking and screaming, and Sean could care less. He stroked the dry walls of my anus, deeper, longer, stronger faster, until I couldn't fight him anymore. Steel barked, damn near trying to fight his way through my back door. He barked, hollered and whimpered, watching through the slightly opened blinds handing over my backdoor. He wanted to help me and couldn't. Sean knew he wouldn't have tried that shit had my Pit been in the house; that's why the nigga put him outside.

"You fuck around with that nigga, you gonna get yourself and that nigga fucked up. No Vaseline, Audrey, just like this! You got that shit?" Sean's breathing was heavy. "It doesn't feel good to you, does it? The shit hurts, don't it?" Sean rested his body on top of mine, slowing his stroke down, his dick stiffening inside of me.

It hurt like a muthafucka. Sean had done a lot of shit to hurt me, but he'd never done anything like this before. He was really pissed at me. I'd apparently overstepped my boundaries. And so had he.

"Fuck you, Sean!" I managed to scream out, despite the fact that he was gripping the shit out of my neck.

Sean gripped my neck, digging his nails into my skin that time, pressing my face into the couch so I really couldn't breathe.

"Nah, I'm fuckin' you! Take this dick, all this shit." Sean hissed in my ear, stroking the shit out of me. He gripped my neck so hard in his hand that he was damn near cutting off my airway.

My screams were muffled by the soft, fluffy cushion of my couch, the couch I would no longer be able to sit in comfortably. I wasn't even sure how long Sean took my shit because I must have passed out twice from the intensity of the pain. All I know was that as soon as Sean climaxed, he pulled out of me and ejaculate on my butt. He slapped his dick on my cheeks, thick fluid dripping down my cheeks.

I cried out loud, my face still buried in the couch. That was until Sean pulled me from the couch by my hair. He turned my body around to face his, and I smacked him dead in his face before he let go of my hair and smacked the fuck out of mine.

I yelled out, about to smack this dude back, when he grabbed me by my forearms. "Get the fuck out, Sean!" I screamed, face throbbing.

"I don't gotta go no muthafuckin' where. You added my name to this got damn lease too, remember? I leave when I choose." Sean slung my ass to the side before walking past me, pulling up his boxers and then his pants.

I cried out, pulling up my panties and then easing my way back into my jeans. My knees were weak; I felt pressure in my chest. I felt like I was about to have a panic attack; I was in so much pain.

"You don't even know this nigga, Audrey, but you wanna work with this muthafucka? The same muthafucka who is the reason I'm not getting paid like I'm supposed to? I produce his shit and come up with these phat ass beats. I write all these songs for this nigga, and he is the mutahfucka who gets all the credit?" Sean yelled out, walking down the hallway.

"No, nigga, I write all the songs!" I cried out, limping behind him.

THE LYRICS TO HIS SONG

Sean stopped in his tracks, turning around to face me. His nostrils flared as he walked up to me, standing before me, eying the side of my face that he'd hit me in. "You wanna repeat that shit?"

"I said that I write the music, Sean. It's about time that I get paid for it! I'm through with you! Get the fuck out!" I pushed him in his chest. "I've known you all my life, and this is how you do me? What kind of man rapes a woman who would give him anything he asked her for? What kind of man takes what's already his? You don't love me! You never did! You come in here, high as fuck off of whatever you don' shot into your veins this time, and you're fuckin' my sister, yet you have the nerve to treat me like shit because I want to do something different with my life than smell muthafuckas feet and watch people try to walk out the got damn store with our new releases? Nigga, you's a bitch! Get the fuck—"

Sean grabbed me by my throat, slamming me into the wall. "Say one more muthafuckin' thing! One more muthafuckin' thing!"

That time, Sean choked me until everything blacked out. When I awoke, I was laying naked in my bed, under the sheets. I was hoping the night before was a dream until I turned over, seeing an open closet with half of the clothes gone out of it. Sean had left; and a part of me did too.

CHAPTER THREE

The Brothers

"You a'ight, boo?" Mariah watched me tagging the new shirts that came in with the truck the next morning.

I felt like someone was sitting on my chest. The pressure had been there ever since what happened the night before with Sean. I needed to go to the hospital, but I refused to go. My heart was already in distress enough. I had gone on ignoring the signs that Sean had lost his mind for years. He'd never violated me or put his hands on me. He was cocky, yes; he was arrogant, but he wasn't abusive. He was really pissed that I wanted to work with Antwan. Up until that point, I thought he and Antwan were friends. But from the moment that Sean saw that I was entering into Antwan's world, he was furious with the entire situation. As far as I knew, Antwan was all about music. He was all about the money. His life was all over the media; it was no secret that the furthest thing from Antwan's mind was a relationship. And if he was ever to get into one, it sure as hell wouldn't have been with me, a girl who didn't have a gangsta bone in her body. But for whatever reason, Sean was threatened by me going anywhere near Antwan or the music industry.

"You've been quiet all morning, hun. You wanna talk about it?" Mariah eyed my profile, watching my eyes water. "What did Sean do this time?"

I didn't say anything; I just kept on tagging. That day, I wore my tinted reading glasses with thick black and white frames made by Chanel. I wore my curly hair clipped to one side so that no one would see the mark that Sean left on my face.

"Well," Mariah sighed. "I found out who Sean was fuckin' with, and it wasn't Brandie."

I looked at Mariah.

Mariah shook her head. "Yeah, I punched that bitch for nothing."

I turned to her, "What you mean?"

Mariah sighed. "So, last night, Fatima dropped me and Elle back off at my crib so that we could change clothes. We planned on stepping out to the club for a few hours before we headed out to Antwan's party. On our way to the club, around like 11:30, I heard something vibrating in my purse. Elle goes through my purse to get the phone. She looks at the phone and was like, 'Boo, why do you have Fatima's phone?' Girl, you already know we're some nosy bitches, and you already know Fatima never keeps a lock on her phone. Soooo…"

I already shook my head to myself because I knew it was about to be some shit.

"Turns out, Sean was texting her! Asking her was she going to the party tonight!" Mariah exclaimed.

I sighed, heart aching in my chest. Man, muthafuckas liked seeing me hurt. I guess my life was just too perfect to them. I hadn't been through enough. Losing a brother wasn't enough. My parents weren't dead, but they hadn't been the same since my brother passed, so it was almost as if I'd lost them too. My entire support system was shattered. All I had were my girls. And that circle was apparently becoming smaller. Fatima used to date my muthafuckin' brother, and now she was fuckin' around with Sean. Guess the bitch was trying to keep it all in the family.

"So, me, being the text-and-drive bitch that I am, I was looking through the phone, trying to see exactly when these two muthafuckas started texting each other. Girl, that shit went all the way back about seven months! I mean, the bitch was on tour with the muthafucka. He didn't bring you with him because he was fuckin' around with her! Sean used your sister as a cover-up to cover up the fact that he was fuckin' around with Fatima!" Mariah watched my fists clench. Mariah shook her head to herself.

"That's not even the worst part of it."

I continued tagging clothes, not really in the mood to hear any more, but with Mariah's mouth, you might as well just chill, sit back, and pop some popcorn because her tell-you-exactly-what-I-saw speeches could go on for hours.

78

"We went to the club and ran into that chick, Brenda. You know, the girl who Antwan was supposed to be dating back in high school. You remember big booty Brenda? Well, you never met her, but you read about that chick in the magazines. Turns out, your man, Sean, got the bitch pregnant a little over four years ago!" Mariah watched me drop the tagging gun.

I looked at Mariah, watching her eyes water. This muthafucka had Antwan's girl pregnant at the same time that I was pregnant. I lost my baby, and he wasn't there for me because the bastard was there for her. I was in an accident that took his baby, and the nigga didn't even give a fuck. Never once felt any sympathy for me for losing my baby. I worked my ass off for years at Foot Locker until I finally became the store manager. I paid all of my bills alone. The only thing Sean ever did for me was bring home expensive shoes and clothes, which the nigga probably got for free from the wardrobe room on the set of Antwan's music videos. The muthafucka was probably in debt because he was paying Brenda to keep quiet. Antwan's girl Brenda.

"Brenda was with Antwan when this nigga got her pregnant, Audrey. This girl grew up with Antwan. From the same hood as Antwan. He did every muthafuckin' thing for this bitch, and she had the nerve to get pregnant by this muthafucka! No wonder why Antwan is on that no-love shit these days! And Sean makes me sick! These bitches are so fuckin' stupid over this nigga!" Mariah was pissed.

I shook my head, bending over to pick up the tagging gun from the floor. "Yeah, apparently I am too."

Mariah shook her head at me, watching me adjust the glasses on my face. "A fool in love, yes. Stupid, no."

"Then why does this shit hurt so bad? It shouldn't hurt this bad! I have known him forever, Mariah! I should have seen these signs! I missed shit that I shouldn't have. There's no way that I should have missed that he has a baby or that he was fuckin' around with my best friend!" I exclaimed.

"He kept you out of the loop. Shit, I was out of the loop, and you know my ass finds out everything!" Mariah rolled her eyes.

"The only reason why Brenda came clean last night is because Sean skipped a child support payment. Oh, best believe this bitch is gonna show up to your rehearsal today. Shit, she showed up to Antwan's man Drizzle's after party last night to confront Sean. And guess who Sean's ass was with?"

I just looked at Mariah.

"Yup, Fatima! We caught the muthafuckas in one of the bedrooms, Sean's hands up the bitch's dress!" Mariah clapped her hands together with each word she spoke. "Girl, I don't even like Brenda, but last night, I helped Brenda get that bitch! Two faces busted in one night over that nigga! I'ma have to apologize to Brandie; she's a hoe, but she wasn't hoeing around with Sean."

My heart pounded in my chest.

"I know Sean's ass showed out when I left last night. I know that nigga came back in Rhymes to confront your ass, huh?" Mariah eyed the hurt expression on my face before pushing my hair from my face.

"What the—?" She pushed my hair back behind my ear and then slowly removed my glasses from my face. She stumbled back a little before tossing my glasses over on top of one of the boxes I still had to open and tag. "What the fuck, Audrey?" Mariah exclaimed, eying the bruises on my neck and left side of my face. "Did Sean do this to your face?"

I snatched my glasses from on top of the box and put my hair back the way that I had it.

"Mariah, leave it alone, okay?"

Mariah's eyes widened. "What? What the fuck happened, Audrey? I ain't leaving shit alone! What happened last night? Aren't you about to go into the studio in a few hours? You're gonna go in that muthafucka with your face looking like this? What do you think Karen is gonna say? Shit, what the fuck do you think Antwan's gonna say? I'm pretty sure the beef that we now know Sean has with Antwan has

Sean feeling some type of way that you're gonna be working with the muthafucka!"

I looked at Mariah. I hadn't told her anything about signing the contract or that I was meeting Antwan and his team that morning. I was sure Antwan told everyone at the after party.

"Yeah, Antwan told us that you signed the contract to work for not Instinctive Entertainment but for his new label, Jewels Entertainment." Mariah's eyes were still glued to my face, still glued to the bruises that I tried to cover.

I nodded. "Yeah, I didn't even read the contract. And apparently Karen didn't either. She thought I was signing with her, but I was signing with Antwan. As soon as I heard I was working for Antwan, I signed that contract. I think a part of me did the shit just to spite Sean."

Mariah nodded in agreement. "Yeah, boo, you've got skills, but I think Antwan signed you just to spite Sean too."

I nodded, sighing. "Yeah, that's what it seems like. Damn." I shook my head. "Brenda's got a baby for real, huh?"

"Yeah, Sean was on that Tupac shit for real." Mariah shook her head.

I looked at her.

She looked at me, a slight grin growing across her face before fading away. "I can't believe that nigga put his hands on you."

82

"That's not all he did, Mariah." I whispered.

"What?" Mariah's eyes searched my face. "What the fuck do you mean, Audrey?"

"Audrey, you asked for me?" I head Korey's voice approaching us before I looked up in the direction that the voice was coming from. Korey Phillips. Well, what could I say about him? He was one of the most ambitious black men that I'd ever met. He was area supervisor, on his way to getting promoted to district supervisor. Rumor had it that he was on his way to launching a line of shoes, that he was entering into an endorsement deal with Adidas. His older brother, Kevin Phillips, played for the Washington Redskins. Korey was just two years older than I was. He was dark skinned with bright brown eyes and perfect white teeth. His hair and face were always cut and trimmed to perfection. He had the perfect build—built as if he was carved in heaven. He was about 6'2'', probably two hundred pounds. He was a sight to see. And he had the biggest crush on me, despite the fact that he was married. Married to a girl I went to school with at that; Adelle McCarthy. He only married her because Sean stood in the way of him trying to marry me. I was a fool in love with Sean, and Korey got tired of waiting. But he did hook me up with a job, a car, and a place to stay, so he didn't entirely forget about me.

"Hey, hey, Korey," I stuttered, glancing at Mariah who was still anxious to know exactly what Sean did to me the night before. I turned to Korey as he walked towards us.

Korey stood before the two of us, eying the clothes that we were tagging. He looked at his watch. "The mall opens in about an hour. Y'all gonna have all of this done by then?"

We both nodded.

"Of course. Elle will be here in about fifteen minutes to help out, Korey." I looked him over, admiring his casual attire. He was dressed perfectly to go out and eat with us. "So, what are your plans for lunch?"

Korey made a face. "Lunch?"

I nodded. "Umm-hmm."

Korey glanced at Mariah and then back at me. "Okay, what's going on? The only time anyone offers to take me to lunch, they're trying to give me some bad news. So, what's up? You quitting on me or what? You might as well just tell me now, Audrey."

"Korey, she was in a talent show last night at the Rhymes! They heard her lyrics, they heard her rap, they heard her sing, and they want her! Well, Antwan does." Audrey nudged me in the side. "She's with Antwan's new label."

84

Korey's eyes lit up just as fast as they dimmed back down. I'd been working with that dude since I was in high school. He had done so much for me. Korey ran his hand over his wavy hair anxiously. "So, what are you saying, Audrey? Today is your last day?"

I hesitated. "And Mariah's too."

Mariah looked at me. I hadn't told her that I told Karen the only way the company was getting me was if they signed her, too. "Wh—what do you mean?" Mariah stuttered.

"I hope you've got your gym bag in the car because practice is at 11:00." I couldn't even get the entire sentence out before Mariah threw her arms around me, knocking my glasses off of my face.

"I'm sorry, boo!" Mariah let go of me, bending over to pick the glasses off the floor.

I turned away from Korey to take the glasses back from her when Korey grabbed my face, turning it towards his.

I cringed at his touch, my jaw aching like a muthafucka.

Korey's temples twitched. "Who the fuck did this shit to your face, Audrey?"

"Sean." Mariah spoke up before I could try to brush the situation off. "That muthafuckin' cheatin' ass, lyin' ass, punk ass Sean. You should've beat his ass back in high school, Korey."

I took Korey's hands from my face. "Are you coming to lunch with us this afternoon or what? I'd really like it if you came, Korey."

Korey shook his head at me. "That nigga has no right to put his hands on you!" Korey wasn't changing the subject. "I told your ass back in high school that you needed to drop that muthafucka and fuck with me, but you wouldn't listen."

"You're married, Korey." I took my glasses from Mariah's hands.

"Yeah," Korey mumbled like he didn't need a reminder that he was married to someone whose spending limit was out of control. "That's beside the point. I wish you all the luck in the world, Audrey; you know I do. I've always been your number one fan."

Mariah cleared her throat, folding her arms.

"Number two. My bad." Korey grinned a little at Mariah before looking back at me. "I already know you didn't call the police, so I don't even have to ask. But all I'm saying is I hope you don't let that nigga get away with this. You're about to work with some ruthless muthafuckas. You need to get one of 'em to take him out. I'm pretty sure he fucked with the wrong nigga's girl; someone will help you get that nigga."

"So," Mariah butted in, "does this mean you're not going with us to lunch? After today, there's no telling when you'll see either one of us. Elle will be here to take over in a few."

Korey looked at me before moving my hair from my face to see the rest of the bruises. He exhaled deeply, his face wrinkling into a frown. "You sure this is what you wanna do, Audrey? You've come a long way from the shy girl you were back in school, but you're not like the other females in that industry."

"I'm just gonna be writing music, Korey. I'm not gonna perform. I did it last night to prove a point to Sean, but I'm not singer or a rapper or a poet. I'm just Audrey, a songwriter." I sighed as Korey ran his fingers over my bruises. "Just let us take you out to lunch. Antwan invited you."

Korey shook his head. "Nah. I don't wanna see you leave me. Mariah, look out for my girl, a'ight? See y'all around." Korey looked at me one last time before turning around to walk out of the store.

***

Mariah's nails damn near dug into my arm as we strolled down the hallway towards the studio where dance rehearsal was being held. A few of Antwan's bodyguards led us in the front and a few more followed close behind us. Man, shit had to be crazy in the industry. I mean, Antwan's bodyguards had bodyguards. I felt like I was in a whole other world as I strolled through Instinctive Studios. They had studios set up in just about every major city in the country, but their sixteen-story building that sat in the middle of downtown Baltimore was their headquarters. I felt like I was in a five-star hotel rather than an office building. There I was, dressed in a jean jacket, white Adidas fitted tee, dark denim skinny jeans, and my fresh white and blue Adidas. Mariah was dressed in a pink crop top, black yoga pants, and pink New Balances. And the bodyguards to the front and behind us were rockin' labels that I couldn't even pronounce.

We stopped in front of the double wooden doors of the dance studio. Two of the bodyguards opened the doors to lead us inside. IEP were scattered throughout the studio, bent over, stretching, getting ready for dance rehearsal. Mickey Clark was the choreographer. She was a bad muthafucka. She once danced for Black Beauty, a well-known dance crew who performed at Howard University. She set off on her own, tired of being in the background, and the rest was dance history. Mariah was still digging her claws into me as we strolled into the studio and damn near passed out at the sight of sought after Mickey Clark.

I rolled my eyes, shaking my head at Mariah. "Can you let go of my arm? You're cutting off my got damn circulation, Mariah!" I whispered to her.

"Oh." Mariah let go of my arm. "My bad."

I rubbed my upper arm, "Damn, witcha' strong ass."

I looked over in the corner where my sister was stretching with her team. I rolled my eyes as they caught sight of us. They all stood up straight, standing there in formation, looking like a black Barbie collection. I laughed to myself as they made their way over to us in the middle of the dance studio. Brandie beat the hell out of her face with Mac makeup to cover up the bruises that Mariah left on her face the night before, but even layers on layers of makeup couldn't cover the scars that Mariah left alongside her eyes and lips.

All nervousness seeped right out of Mariah as soon as she was confronted by the group of females that she had absolutely no respect for. She'd seen them do too much and end up with so little. There were only a select few dancers who ended up in videos; the rest might as well call themselves groupies because they sure didn't go on the road with the company other than as sex objects. I have to give it to them; they danced hard. But they sucked dick harder. No one took their asses seriously. The only reason why Brandie even made it as far as she did was because her mother, Odessa Wrigley, was head prosecutor for the states attorneys' office downtown. She was the reason why half of the artists that worked for the company weren't in jail. Yeah, Brandie sucked a lot of dick, just like her teammates, but what set her apart was that she had the hook-up for those who needed a get-out-of-jail-free card.

"Look at this stupid hoe, with a whole herd of even stupider hoes backing her up." Mariah nudged me. "Well," Mariah sighed, "It seems as though I owe your bitch ass an apology. You're a hoe, that's for damn sure, but you weren't hoeing around with Sean."

Brandie rolled her eyes a little, glancing at me. She knew she wished she had a friend like Mariah, who would never hesitate to defend her bestie at the drop of a dime. All Brandie's friends did was talk shit, hoping the next bitch would be too afraid to confront their ass. But those of us who knew them knew that they were all bark with no got-damn bite.

Brandie looked at me. "The next time you go out, Audrey, you need to make sure you have your dog," she glanced at Mariah, "on a leash."

Mariah laughed out loud, about to lay hands on Brandie again before I pulled her away.

"Chill, Mariah!" I squealed. "I got you in, boo, so you need to make sure you stay your ass out of trouble!" I reminded Mariah as she pulled away from me. "We both know the reason why Brandie is hatin' right now. I used word of mouth to get you in, where as she used her mouth in other ways to get to where she is today. Which is nowhere but dancing on the set of videos before she's fuckin' and suckin' niggas off the set of music videos."

Brandie scoffed, folding her arms.

I still didn't put shit past her. Sean wasn't giving her jewelry for nothing. She was doing him some type of favor. I just didn't know what it was yet. She must have known something that apparently he didn't want her to tell.

Brandie looked me over. "Audrey, I don't even know why you're over here trippin' off that nigga. Don't nobody want Sean but you. Oh, and Brenda."

Brandie's friends giggled behind her.

"Shit, and that friend you're always defending, fake-ass Fatima." Brandie smirked.

I glared at Brandie.

"I hate to be the bearer of bad news, but Brenda trapped ya nigga. Did you know she has a baby with Sean? Their baby's birthday is May 25th, 2013. But hold up, isn't that the same due date the doctors gave you when you were pregnant?" Brandie grinned.

If Mariah hadn't stepped in between the two of us, I swear, she would have had bruises on the right side of her face to match the left.

"A'ight, Brandie, you're crossing the line. I suggest you shut the fuck up before you get smacked the fuck up. You're dirty as hell for bringing that shit up! That was your niece or got-damn nephew that was killed in that crash, muthafucka! That was your got-damn brother, too, who died in that crash, and you're standing here making jokes about the shit just to hurt your sista!" Mariah snarled at Brandie, who had no heart to care about anything that Mariah was saying.

Brandie rolled her eyes to fight off any emotion that she may have felt about the fatal car crash. "All I'm saying is don't nobody want that muthafucka like she thinks they do. Shit, she shouldn't even want the muthafucka. I swear, I never touched that nigga, and I don't want to neither. That nigga is broke as fuck, which is the only reason why he's going over to work for Relentless. He doesn't know he's about to do some of everything to get that money. Ain't no telling what type of hoes he's about to be fuckin' with now, Audrey. Fuck Sean. You need to be worried about who's fuckin' with Antwan. That's the nigga I'm checkin' for."

I just looked at Brandie, feeling like snatching all that pretty sleek black hair from her scalp, right from the roots.

"Who wants a cheeseburger when I can have a juicy ass, Tuscan, sirloin steak?" Brandie scoffed.

"Girl, you're trippin'. You know Sean's meat is juicy than a muthafucka too!" Brandie's teammate, Julie, high-fived another dancer.

I had had enough. I had to walk away before I beat one of them bitches. I knew Sean was so not worth fighting over, but the blatant disrespect was what made me want to beat the shit out of my sister and her friends.

Brandie grabbed my arm before I could walk away. "Awe, don't be like that. They were only joking."

I tried pulling from her, but she wouldn't let go of my arm.

She looked into my face before letting go of my arm. And she slid my glasses from my face. It was the first time that my sister actually looked me in the face with any type of remorse. It didn't last long though.

Mariah snatched the glasses from Brandie's hands and gave them back to me. I couldn't cover my face with makeup the way that Brandie did. I was allergic to any and everything. The only makeup I wore was mascara and lipstick.

"What the fuck happened to her face, Mariah?" Brandie glanced at Mariah and then back at me.

"Oh, what do you care? Y'all are over here, cracking jokes and shit about the girl." Mariah snapped on Brandie.

"Sean did this shit to her, didn't he? I told Audrey from the jump not to fuck with that nigga! That he was no good! And that was way before the fame, way before he made a name for himself in the industry, way before the hoes, way before the cheating, and apparently way before he thought it was cool to put his got-damn hands on her! That must be the type of shit she likes though because she's still with the nigga." Brandie folded her arms, looking me over. "Too afraid to venture off on her own and leave that nigga behind. That was a cute little song you did last night. Too bad you didn't mean it. You talked all that shit and still got the nerve to accept that nigga's engagement ring."

Mariah and I looked at one another and then back at Brandie.

Brandie eyed the clueless expression on both of our faces.

"He announced your engagement this morning on the radio, on 95.5."

I stumbled back. "What?"

"Yeah, he mentioned y'all having an engagement party next weekend. I'm like, boy, that was quick. I thought she told the nigga to pack his shit." Brandie shook her head at me.

Man, my head was spinning. I was in a daze that afternoon, sitting across from Karen in her office, as her assistant explained the paperwork that I would be signing. I couldn't believe that after everything Sean did to me the night before that he would have the audacity to broadcast an engagement over the airwaves. Everyone had got wind of the supposed engagement. He was trying to prove a point to Antwan. Trying to prove that, no matter how much he mistreated me, he still owned me. That I would still run back to the nigga. As soon as I sat across from Karen that day in her office, she slid the gray velvet box across the table to me. Inside was the most beautiful engagement ring. I remember my father buying my mother a similar ring back when I was in middle school. My mother was into all types of jewelry, especially anything made by Tiffany & Co. Anything she wanted from that jewelry store, Daddy's guilt about the things he took her through would make him go out and get it for her. She came home one day with the prettiest patented cushion-cut Tiffany diamond ring. The diamond was surrounded by bead-set diamonds. The white-gold ring was so shiny that it almost appeared to be sky blue. The ring was an apology gift my father had given her after a huge fight they'd had the night before, after a woman called the house, telling my mother that she was pregnant. And there I was, sitting at Karen's desk that day, looking at basically the same got-damn ring.

I huffed, gazing at the ring. As pretty as it was, it symbolized something that I hated. I didn't have the worst childhood, but I sure as hell didn't have the best. My father was an awesome father when it came to taking care of his children and spending time with us, but as far as a husband, he should have been fired.

"That is a beautiful ring." Karen's assistant, Vita-Jean, eyed me staring down at the ring.

"But, why is it in your box and not on your finger?"

I laughed a little, looking up at Vita-Jean. "I was wondering the same damn thing." I looked at Karen.

Karen shook her head at me like I must have been crazy not to consider the fact that Sean was proposing to me to be the best news I'd received all day. "Sean Lee is proposing to you. I repeat, Sean Lee is proposing to you! Sean Lee is about to bring this company millions! A.J. Miller asked me to sign you because of your affiliation with Sean. Antwan has his own reasons for wanting to work alongside you, but my agenda includes money. Yours should too. When a nigga like Sean Lee wants you to do whatever, you do it."

"Sean Lee ain't shit, Karen!" I took the glasses from my face, tossing them on the table.

Both of the two looked at me, eyes tracing the bruises that lined my jawbone and ear.

"Ummm." Vita-Jean tried to stay out of my business and continue getting me prepared to work with the company. "Here is your iPhone, iPad, and iWatch." She slid over three brand new electronic devices that I should have been happy about, but I wasn't at the moment.

"Karen, would you marry a muthafucka who smacked you in the face? Who held you down and raped you in the ass, no Vaseline?" I squealed, telling Karen something I hadn't said out loud to anyone yet.

Karen gasped a little.

Vita-Jean's eyes widened before she went back to organizing the paperwork that she had me sign that morning. She didn't know what to say. I think she was actually afraid to say anything.

"Sean Lee raped me, and I'm supposed to take this ring as an apology gift, Karen? Would you?" I exclaimed.

Karen took a deep breath. "Sean was drunk and high out of his mind last night. I told you not to go home to him, didn't I? Those niggas that he hangs with do all types of hallucinogens! I'm sure Sean doesn't even remember what he did to you!"

I couldn't believe she was making excuses for him. "Karen, okay, so if he didn't know what the fuck he did to me, why is he proposing to me with a ring that his ass can't even afford?"

"He's been talking about proposing to you for months now, Audrey!" Karen defended him. "He's working with A.J. Miller just so he can afford to pay for this ring!"

"Did you know that he had a baby with Brenda Morris?" I asked.

Karen was reluctant to nod her head, but she did. "Yes."

"Did you know that the baby was born the same day that my baby was supposed to be born?" I whispered.

Karen nodded, her eyes sparkling. "Yes, honey, I did. But that's all water under the bridge now. It's over with Brenda. He pays her child support; he spends time with his kids—"

I interrupted her. "Whoa, wait a minute now! Kids? What got-damn kids?"

Karen sighed, leaning back in his chair. "Fatima's two-year-old son, Quan."

I laughed out loud to keep from crying out. When I saw Fatima's face, I was going to fuck her ass up. "Does Snare know about this?"

Karen shook her head. "Of course not, and you need to pretend that you don't know either. That's their business."

"No, Karen, it's mine!" I squealed.

"No, what's your business is this." Karen pointed to the stack of paperwork that Vita-Jean held in her hands. "You're about to be rich. No more struggling. No more worries. Marry Sean and ignore his bullshit. I'm sorry about what he did to you, but you can't even imagine the shit that I've been through with Ervin. The niggas in this industry do us dirty, but that's the life that we chose. They mistreat us, they cheat on us, they beat on us, and yes, sometimes they violate us. But at least the nigga you're with hasn't let his friends have sex with you, whichever way that they like, just to pay off of his debts!"

Vita-Jean and I both looked at her.

"I can't tell you how many niggas he let up in our house to rape me! You're crying because your boyfriend had sex with you a little too rough? Try the loan sharks, the realtor, gang leaders, other musicians, drug dealers, hit men, my own got-damn father-in-law!" Karen wiped the tears that escaped from her pretty brown eyes. "Sean was high as a got-damn kite when he did that to you! Has he ever put his hands on you before? Has he ever raped you before?"

I hesitated. "That's not the point, Karen!"

THE LYRICS TO HIS SONG

"It is the fuckin' point, Audrey! When you see him today, I guarantee you that he's not going to remember he did this shit to your face or whatever else he did to hurt you! I promise you! That ring isn't an apology gift from last night. It may be a guilt ring from the other shit he's done, but it's not from what he did last night. Chuck the shit up, and move the fuck on, Audrey." Karen sat up in her chair.

And I leaned back in mine, pissed because I knew that once I told my mother what happened to me, she was going to give me the exact same speech. So, I decided that those two were going to be the only ones who knew the truth about what Sean did to me.

"Now, you were supposed to be here early this morning. Antwan has been in the studio all day working with his brother. His brother works with Trey Benson at BAM Inc., ugh. Apollo would be a perfect addition to our label, but unfortunately, we can't offer him the perks that BAM can." Karen huffed, sliding me more documents to sign.

"Antwan told me to come in at 11:00. Said that I should take my manager out to lunch after rehearsal, but my manager refused. He wasn't too happy to see me go. Korey has done so much to help me, unlike the nigga whose proposal you're telling me to accept." I watched Karen rolling her eyes.

"Anyway," Karen pursed her lips at me, "I hope you brought a few songs for Antwan to work on today. I'm trying to get this nigga away from gangsta rap for this next album. I want him to cross over into the pop world, and I know you're just the one to help me. I heard this nigga singing one day down in one of his houses. He says he has a piano that I never knew that he had. This dude wrote a song for his mama, Audrey. I want you to get him to sing it to you. You have his mama's heart inside of you; I'm sure he'd do anything for you."

I looked at her, my anger subsiding a little.

"Drizzle, Snare, Apollo, and Antwan are in the studio right now. I invited Queen Gates over." Karen watched my eyes widen a little. Karen grinned. "After finding out that you won the contest last night and accepted the position, she agreed to come work for Antwan as your vocal coach."

I shook my head, "Whoa, wait, hold up. I was hired as Antwan's songwriter. I'm not a singer. I just looked over the contract this morning. The terms of the contract were that I write for Antwan, and that's it. It didn't say anything about singing hooks or—"

Karen cut me off. "You can write hooks though, right? Well, then your ass can sing 'em, too. You are very talented Mrs. Audrey Gibson-Lee. Don't underestimate yourself. Don't sell yourself short. We can draft up another contract. You can be his songwriter, and you can be my singer."

I shook my head. "The stage isn't where I belong, Karen."

THE LYRICS TO HIS SONG

"Haven't you been behind the scenes long enough, Audrey?" Karen reminded me. "Just think about it."

***

"Bullets flying over top of you; you dropped your gun, what you gonna do? Shouldn't have fucked with the Royal crew; you stomped on our ground, we gon' murder you. Kidnap your bitch and your daughter, too; you fired shots, we gon' fire, too. Put the dick in her mouth, right in front of you; you asked for this shit, now enjoy the view..." I watched Apollo and Antwan spit lyrics through the mic, behind the soundproof glass of the recording booth.

Drizzle sat in front of the equipment, head bopping to the music and the lyrics flowing through the twins' mouth. Queen Gates stood alongside the wall. Snare stood beside her, hands moving as if he was pretending to play drums to the beat of the music. I wasn't gonna lie; the lyrics that flowed from their lips was phenomenal. A little intimidating, but that was what gangsta rap was. Every other word that came from their lips drilled into your soul. They spoke on everything from killing their rival's entire family to having sex with their rival's girl while their rival watched the shit. I was blown away. My heart leaped in my chest to the beat of the music that flowed around us.

Antwan signaled Drizzle to stop the music once he caught sight of me stepping into the studio, closing the door behind me.

Apollo looked up at me. Apollo had a pecan brown complexion with light eyes and brown dreads. He rocked purple from the purple baseball cap on his head to the purple bandana draped around his neck to that crisp Giuseppe plaid shirt to the purple high-top Giuseppe's housing his feet. Antwan, on the other hand, was dressed in "The Hood Raised Me" apparel, a clothing line created by the two brothers. Antwan wore all black; even his Gucci watch was dripping in black gold. Though the brothers weren't identical, that smile of theirs was the same. That little conniving, manipulative, yet adorably irresistible smile.

"What's up, Lyric?" Antwan greeted me as he stepped out of the booth with Apollo following close behind him, brown dreads shining under the studio lights.

I eyed the nine millimeters that both had tucked in their jeans. As a matter-of-fact, Drizzle, Snare, and Queen were strapped too. I looked back up at the twins. I felt like I was walking through the hood as I strolled down the hallway that afternoon to the studio. Every hood nigga that Apollo knew was chillin' in the hallway.

"The whole hood is in the place, I see." I had to comment.

Everyone chuckled a little.

"Y'all know I don't go anywhere without my hittas." Apollo looked me over, gold grill gleaming. "You know niggas always actin' strange. Pops got his niggas around here lurkin' and shit. I don't trust that nigga." Apollo looked into my face. "So, what do you think about my new single, The Right One? It's hittin', huh?"

Antwan looked at me.

They all looked at me.

I swallowed hard, spotlight on me. "It was alright, I guess."

Antwan laughed out loud as the cocky expression disappeared from his brother's face.

"A'ight? Fuck you mean it was just 'a'ight?'" Apollo felt some type of way about me and my worthless-ass opinion.

I shrugged. "I mean, it's just so… ruthless. So… hood."

"Shit, we're some ruthless, hood muthafuckas." Antwan laughed at me.

I sighed. "Try something different for a change, huh; that's all I'm saying. Why don't you try raping about something other than shooting and killing?"

"That's all I know, Lyric." Antwan shrugged. "Shit, that's all any gansta knows."

"Try rapping about love." I suggested.

"I never knew anything about love." Antwan seemed ashamed to say.

His brother, Apollo, nodded in agreement. "Hell nah."

"Ok, Antwan, Apollo... Rap about that." I grinned a little, hoping someday I'd be blessed to teach him.

"I don't know, Ma." Antwan wasn't so sure.

"Well, think about it. I mean, that entire song is about killing a dude after making him watch you both have sex with his baby mama." I watched the twins give each other dap. I rolled my eyes at their ignorance before spitting a few lyrics from their song that I remembered. "'Body pumped full of lead, took 'bout fifty shots to the head. The last sight that you saw, was my dick in your bitch, me fuckin' her raw.'" I was disgusted that I even knew the lyrics to the song and even more disgusted that Apollo was proud of the lyrics to that song. "Apollo, did you write that triflin' shit?"

Apollo frowned a little, laughter fading quickly. "Yo, where you from, Ma?"

"I was born in Florida, but lived in Maryland all of my life. I was raised in Hanover, right outside of Fort Meade, in the Provinces before Dad got a better job, and we moved out to Columbia." I looked around at everyone who was looking at me.

"Okay." Apollo nodded, grinning. "Which neighborhood?" He looked me over. "Your daddy is a lawyer, right? Your mom works for the Library of Congress? Yeah, you probably lived off of Harpers Farm Road, huh?"

I nodded. "Yes, as a matter-of-fact, we moved there when I was in the ninth grade."

"You had both parents in your life, huh? Who both had high paying jobs and shit. Daddy probably came back home to Mama every night at 6:00. Probably had an office in the basement where he did all of his work. I'm pretty sure y'all ate together like one big happy family every night, huh? Mama in her lil' white apron; Daddy still in his suit and tie. Mama probably ironed his clothes, draws, and the nigga's socks. Daddy gave you everything you ever asked for, made sure his princess didn't want for anything. Didn't he?" Apollo scoffed, gritting his teeth.

I folded my arms, resenting the fact that he thought he knew me. "You don't know shit about my life, Apollo."

"And you don't know shit about ours to call our lyrics triflin' either, shawty." Antwan defended his brother.

I looked at Antwan. "Do y'all have any idea of how many siblings I have outside of Brandie? My father had six children while he was married to my mother! Does that sound like a happy marriage to you?"

Everyone in the studio laughed a little.

"Are you serious right now?" Snare muttered to himself. "I wish cheat was all my got-damn father did. I grew up in the back of a crack house. My father was a pimp. I lived with my father and about fifteen other women, and my dad had at least two children by each and every last one of them hoes."

My eyes widened a little before I exhaled deeply.

"Shit, my father beat the shit out my mother just about every day." Drizzle spoke up. "One night, he beat the shit outta Moms because she cooked Kraft Macaroni and Cheese instead of Velveeta Shells and Cheese. He beat her so bad that he knocked her right eye out of its socket. Mom went to sleep that night and never woke up the next morning. Before my dad could get arrested for what he did to my mom, he shot himself in the head at the breakfast table, in front of me, my little sister, and little brother. My brother was six years old at the time; my little sister was two."

We all shook our heads to ourselves.

"We've seen some shit that we shouldn't have seen at a very young age. Shit that your spoiled eyes couldn't even imagine. The shit I've been through would have killed you or at least killed your spirit, shawty. You think the shit we spit is too hood. Nah, shawty, the shit we spit is too real." Antwan's eyes sparkled under the studio lights.

"Did you know Queen Gates is our cousin?" Apollo nodded his head towards my favorite local poet and songstress.

I looked at Queen.

She winked at me, her thick, natural hair sitting on top of her head like a crown.

"When her mama—my Aunt Pam, died of a drug overdose, Uncle Walter took her in and raised her in an apartment right next door to Grandma's. You have no idea how many times my uncle sold her to feed his crack habit. I can't tell you how many times he kidnapped us from Grandma's house and tried to sell us for sex to all types of dealers and rich muthafuckas!" Antwan exclaimed. "My uncle sold me to this rich white couple when I was just eight-years-old. As soon as that nigga's pants came down in front of me, I tried to cut that nigga's dick off! Once Grandma died, Uncle Walter and his twin, Clyde, who lived at Grandma's apartment, raised us. They beat the shit out of us every chance that they got. I took hundreds of beatings for Queen; everything she did wrong, they were going upside her head. Once, the nigga shaved her bald because she snuck out one night to be with this dude who lived in Pioneer City."

"Uncle Dante, their older brother, was this big time drug dealer years ago before he was ratted out and sent to the Feds." Apollo continued the story. "He was the entire reason that Uncle Walter was strung out on drugs the way that he was. When Uncle Dante came over and saw the bruises that were all over all three of us, he took us from Uncle Walter and moved us in with one of his girlfriends who lived a few blocks away in Meade Village. Shit, living with Sasha wasn't any better. Once Uncle Dante was arrested, Sasha had us doing everything to help maintain the lifestyle that Uncle Dante had her living. Had Queen selling drugs and sex for her. Had us dealing and killing for her. We were twelve years old then."

"When I went to juvenile detention at the age of twelve, that's when I met the mayor." Antwan told us. "She came in my room, sat down, and talked to me for hours. I felt like I'd known her forever. I felt like there was finally someone who understood my pain. She cared about what I was talking about, and she actually listened. She gave me her number and told me to call her any time. She told me that she was sorry about the life that I lived, but it was up to me to make a change. That I wasn't the person that I showed everyone else. That I was a good boy. That she believed in me. When she left, my counselor called me to her office. Ol' girl was like, 'oh, I see your mother stopped by to see you today.'" Antwan shook his head to himself. "Up until that point, I was told my mother was dead. Grandma never talked about our mother, except to say that she'd taken us from our mother because our mother couldn't love us. I met the mayor that one day and never saw her again until I saw her lying in her casket, four years ago."

"Yeah." Apollo nodded, temples twitching. "And I didn't find out the nigga, A.J. Miller, was my father until I had the nigga at gunpoint the night of Mom's funeral. I visited Uncle Dante that day in prison. He told me that night that Mom gave us up because our father raped her. When I asked him who our father was, he told me it was A.J. Miller. When I saw that nigga at Mom's funeral service, yeah, I pulled a gun on the nigga in church. Been beefin' with the nigga ever since. As soon as I see that nigga's face in this building, I'ma get that nigga, too."

Antwan shook his head at his brother. "Nah, nigga, let the shit go. Stay away from that nigga. You know the power that nigga has. Before you can get one bullet in him, there will be ten nigga's aiming at'cha ass. Mama didn't give a fuck, Pops didn't give a fuck; nigga, it is what it is. Just let the shit go. Fuck."

I looked at Antwan, watching his nose flaring. I could feel his pain; his mother's heart thumping inside of me with every word her sons spoke.

"So." Apollo changed the subject. I felt his eyes tracing my profile, watching me looking at his brother. "Now you know why we spit the lyrics that we spit. So, tell me more about you. Bruh says you're the recipient of our mother's heart."

I hesitated, looking at Apollo and then back at his brother. "Ummm... Yeah." I looked back at Apollo.

Apollo nodded. "A'ight, that's what's up. You're all we have left of her, all we'll ever know of her. Her blood runs through your veins, too, so you're family now, shawty. Our little sister. So you know we're gonna look out for you." Apollo nudged me in my arm.

Drizzle sat at the equipment, a mid-tempo beat flowing through the speakers around us. Drizzle was from the West Coast, so just about everything he mixed together reminded you of The Chronic album. But that day, he threw a little Chesapeake Bay into the mix. Queen hummed to the beat. Snare started beating on the wall like he was beating on his set of drums.

"So, what'cha got for us, Ma? Since you said we're too 'hood' and shit, lemme hear what you came up with. None of that Keith Sweat, Jodeci, Chris Brown, all-we've-got-is-fifteen-minutes, fuck-you-back-to-sleep,let's-make-sweet-love-til-the-muthafuckin'-morning shit either." Antwan shook his head at me, standing alongside his brother. "Gimme something I can relate to. Something that pays homage to the struggle."

Everyone focused their attention on me, to see what I could come up with at the drop of a dime. Like I was a freestyler or some shit.

I hated being put on the spot, but after hearing everyone talking about their life that day in the studio, I already had an R&B version of their life in my head.

I cleared my throat before rapping the first bar of the lyrics to his song. "The streets were my father; the game was my mother. Only one I could call on was Apollo, my brother. Never knew my mom, can give two fucks 'bout my dad. Don't know shit about love, something I never had. Don't ask me shit about love, all I know is the hustle. I grew up in the hood, all I know is the struggle."

I watched everyone grinning at my no-way-near-finished song.

"Something like that, ya know?" I looked around at everyone.

"It still tells your story without someone getting murdered in the process."

Antwan's eyes squinted a little, looking my face over the same way that my sister was a little while earlier. I sighed as Antwan's hand grazed against my neck as he pushed my hair to the side, away from my face. He looked back at his brother before taking my Chanel glasses from my face.

I exhaled deeply, watching Antwan sit down in the leather chair behind him. "Can I have my glasses back please, Antwan?"

"Got damn!" Queen stood up straight from the wall, making her way over to me, looking my face over too. "That nigga tattooed your face with his hand!"

Antwan frowned a little, clearing his throat before rapping.

"So, let me tell you 'bout this beautiful girl, about the day Audrey Gibson stepped into my world. Just when I thought all hope was gone, she stepped on that stage, put all she had into that song. It seems she's in love with a user; all the nigga ever does is abuse her. She's got some nerve tryin'a tell me about love; when her nigga's out there fuckin' hoes, raw, doesn't bother using a glove."

I scoffed, about to walk away when Antwan grabbed my arm. I looked at him, eyes full of tears.

"So, what was it you said about singing about love, shawty?" Apollo laughed a little.

"Shit, seems like you don't know shit about love either." Antwan shook his head at me, letting go of my arm.

"You want me to get that nigga for you, shawty?" Apollo snarled. "I never liked that nigga anyway, especially since he started fuckin' around with Brenda. My brother did any and everything for that girl and she—"

"Shawty," Antwan cut his brother off. "You really about to marry this nigga? I was at the radio station early this morning with the nigga when he announced that shit. I told the radio host that I'd just signed you to my new record label, and then Sean had to let 'em know that he proposed to you last night. Are you really that stupid, Lyric?"

I backed away from him.

"Excuse me, has anyone seen Sean?" I heard an unfamiliar voice over my shoulder. I saw Queen rolling her eyes and smacking her lips at whoever it was over my shoulder before I turned around to see this cute, shapely, brown-skinned girl. She was a petite little thing, but she had curves and an ass on her that was out of this world. I thought my sister was the baddest chick as far as looks were concerned, but Brenda looked like she jumped straight out of King Magazine. The bitch was so flawless that she almost looked airbrushed.

Antwan stood from the chair he was sitting in when he saw her, his temples twitching. "The fuck you doin' in here?"

Brenda glanced at me and then back at Antwan. "I'm looking for Sean. Have you seen him? He's supposed to be taking Lil' Sean to the movies this afternoon."

"Nah, I ain't seen the muthafucka." Antwan snarled. "Ask his fiancé here; maybe she's seen him. Audrey, have you seen your man? He has all these bitches rollin' up in my studio lookin' for him and shit."

Brenda scoffed. "Fiance? Since when?" She looked me over.

"Since I proposed to bae last night." Sean came strolling into the studio, closing the door behind him.

I rolled my eyes, backing up a little, almost backing into Antwan. I looked back at him and then at Sean as he strolled over to me, pulling me away from Antwan by my wrist.

I looked up at Sean as his eyes searched my face.

Sean frowned, looking my face over. "What the fuck happened to your face, yo? Who'd you get in a fight with?" Sean pushed my hair to the side to get a better view of the bruises that he left on my face.

I pulled from Sean. "Are you serious?" I laughed a little.

Sean didn't see anything funny. He looked at Brenda and then back at me. "What happened, Audrey? Tell me who did this shit to you, so I can handle the shit now!"

I shook my head at him. "You—You really don't remember what happened last night?"

"I was faded like a muthafucka last night." Sean laughed to himself. "I don't remember shit last night. The last thing I remember is your girl smacking the fuck out of Brandie because she thought we were fuckin' around."

I looked at Brenda, shaking my head at her. "Well, looks like my girl smacked the wrong trick." I looked at Snare, wanting to mention Fatima's name, but I didn't. "Turns out you were fuckin' around with Brenda. Turns out you have children that I never knew about. Turns out the baby you have with Brenda was born the same day that our baby would have been born if I wouldn't have lost our baby in that car accident!" I pushed Sean in his chest. "You have some nerve smacking the shit out of me and violating me, when you went and had not one but two kids on me."

114

Sean was more focused on the incident I was talking about instead of what he had done outside of our relationship. "Wait, hold up; smacked you? Violated you? When the fuck did this happen? Were you sleepwalking again?"

I pushed Sean. "Are you serious? Sean—" I stopped talking, looking around at everyone. Antwan and Apollo looked like they were ready to unload a few bullets on Sean. Snare, Drizzle, and Queen looked curious to know what two babies I was referring to.

I looked back at Sean. "How could you not tell me about those kids? How could you do this to me? Brenda, weren't you Antwan's girl? What the fuck were you doing with my man?"

Brenda grinned. "Your nigga? Bitch, this is our nigga! Our nigga pays my rent, our nigga puts food on my table, our nigga takes care of my baby, our nigga buys my clothes, and our nigga sleeps with me every got-damn night! This nigga has gotten money out of your bank account to do for me and my kids, bitch! This here is our nigga!"

I went to lunge at her, but Sean pulled me back. I snatched from him, Brenda laughing her ass off.

"Brenda, you need to get the fuck out of here before you getcha ass beat." Queen warned her. "Me and you already done got into it several times. You need to get'cha life and stop fuckin' with every nigga in Antwan's crew."

"Brenda," Sean shoved Brenda, "why you coming in here, starting shit? You know we ain't fucked around in years, Ma. You're just fuckin' with my girl because you must've heard my announcement on the radio this morning. Is that it?"

Brenda rolled her eyes. "What announcement? The one where you were frontin' because Antwan got'cha girl working for him? The announcement you made because you know Antwan is about to snatch your girl from you? You put a ring on that bitch because you didn't want that nigga to snatch that bitch, and you know it. Let's be real."

Apollo smirked.

Sean frowned. "What the fuck do you want? I told you not to come by here."

"You promised to take our son to the movies today, Sean. And you're late on the child support payment. Brandie's momma has gotten you out of a lot of trouble, but a criminal lawyer is no good to you in juvenile court. You want me to bring the white man into this shit? I will, Sean. You marry this bitch, and I swear, I'ma take you for everything you and this bitch are about to make. You just watch and see." Brenda smacked her lips at Sean before she looked at Snare. "Hey, Snare. When you see Fatima, ask her how her eye feels. Last time I saw her; Mariah's fist was in it." Brenda looked back at Sean, who shut his mouth real quick. "You don't remember anything from last night, huh? Do you remember why Fatima got her ass beat? Snare, did you know that your girl—"

Snare looked at Sean and then back at Brenda. "The fuck? What's going on with Fatima? Shawty was supposed to go out of town last night. When the fuck did y'all see Fatima?"

"Ask Sean, Snare!" Brenda yelped as Sean snatched her ass by her arm, tossing her ass towards the door.

"Get the fuck on with that bullshit, Brenda. Get the fuck outta here," Sean growled at her. "Say something else, Brenda."

Brenda stuck her middle finger up at Sean. "Or what, nigga? You ain't gonna do shit! Ain't nobody scared of your ass but little Audrey. Come pick up your son, or I'll be dropping him off on Audrey's doorstep, muthafucka." She blew both of us a kiss before she turned around, walking towards the door."

I exhaled deeply, looking up at Sean as he eyed Brenda walking out the door.

"Bruh, you need to keep your bitches in line and outta my got-damn studio." Antwan gritted his teeth. "She ain't welcome here, and as far as I'm concerned, anyone affiliated with A.J. Miller ain't allowed in my shit either. You can get the fuck on too. Go follow your bitch. Fuck that shit Ervin and Karen are talkin' about. I made this company; they didn't."

Sean shook his head at Antwan. "As long as my girl is here, nigga, I'm here." Sean looked back at me. "We're having lunch with your parents' tomorrow at 12:30." Sean shut me up before I could say anything. "Mama flew in from Texas this morning. You know she just bought that house in Richmond, so we'll be seeing a lot of her. I'm about to drive down to Richmond to go pick her up. Meet me over your parent's crib tomorrow, a'ight?" Sean kissed me on the cheek and left me standing there in the studio looking stupid as hell. As usual.

"I told you let me take that muthafucka out, shawty." Apollo shook his head.

"Man, fuck that nigga." Antwan growled. "Let's go eat."

CHAPTER FOUR

Come and Talk to Me

Rhandy, Antwan's best friend and head of security, took us out for lunch at Carolina Kitchen in North East Washington, D.C. Apollo didn't roll with us. He left with his boys to handle some business in Severn. I rode in the back of a stretch Rolls Royce Phantom Limo with Antwan, Queen, Rhandy, Mariah, Vita-Jean, Drizzle, and Snare. About four bodyguards led us to the front, in their Navigator; and four bodyguards followed closely behind us in theirs. Before we went in the restaurant, the bodyguards went inside to make sure it was safe. Seems as though Antwan's head was wanted everywhere. Seemed like he had to watch his back everywhere that he went.

"Welcome, welcome, welcome!" The staff at the restaurant greeted us as we strolled into the restaurant.

I was so hungry, in a daze looking at the food behind the glass as the workers prepared my plate. I was going to fuck that food up. I was so nervous that entire day that I hadn't eaten anything. Not to mention, I was afraid to eat anything that was going to make me shit after what Sean did to me. And as soon as I thought about him shoving that dick through me, my appetite was gone.

"Girl, I am about to fuck this muthafuckin' chicken up!" Mariah grabbed my arm that day, next to me in line. "Mickey worked the fuck outta your girl today in practice. Do you hear me? I showed every last one of them bitches up today at rehearsal!" Mariah nudged me, twerkin' just a little.

I grinned at her. "I already know how you do, boo. You ain't gotta tell me you killed them bitches."

Mariah grinned. "Damn right. You should have seen Brandie's hatin' ass when I auditioned for the lead in the last single for Antwan's album, The Pole. Brandie just knew that she had the part. Bitch thought just because a bitch doesn't take pipe that I couldn't climb one!"

I burst out laughing, glancing at Antwan who was laughing with his homeboys about five people down from me.

Mariah glanced at him, too.

The both of us got quiet, slick eavesdropping in on Antwan's conversation with Rhandy.

"So-called engaged or not, there's something about that girl." Antwan glanced at me, really not giving a damn if I heard the fool talking about me.

"You're trippin', Twan. You know that's Sean's girl." Rhandy shook his head at Antwan.

Antwan scoffed. "The fuck does that have to do with me?"

Queen cleared her throat. "Ummm, Cuz, you gonna pick out something to eat or are you gonna talk about something that you have no chance at having? A bitch is hungry, got damn, hurry up!"

The line chuckled a little. I was embarrassed out of my mind. He was too bold and didn't give a fuck.

"No chance my muthafuckin' ass. She's here, ain't she? She's still breathing, ain't she? She saw that ring in Karen's office and left the muthafucka sitting on Karen's desk, didn't she? Did she put the muthafucka on? Don't try to play me, Queen. I don't give a damn what y'all say. By the time we head out on tour, I guarantee she'll be in love with a nigga." Antwan boldly told everyone listening in line that afternoon.

"Oh my goodness." I blushed, looking away from him.

When we went to sit down at the booths, there was no room for me. There was a high-top in the corner of the dining area. I shrugged, making my way over to the table.

"Hold up, boo; I'll sit witcha." Mariah picked up her tray of food, about to walk over to me, when Antwan signaled her to have a seat.

"Nah, I'll sit with shawty." Antwan grinned, walking over to the table as I hopped into the chair.

"Oh my God." I mumbled to myself as Antwan came over and sat his food and drink on the table, sitting across from me. His plate looked so healthy compared to mine. He had fish, shrimp, rice, corn, mashed potatoes, and corn bread. I, on the other hand, had two ribs, two fried chicken legs, two barbequed chicken legs, a slice of ham, mac and cheese, baked beans, coleslaw, a biscuit, and a piece of cornbread. Oh, and a piece of chocolate cake.

"Got-damn!" Antwan laughed, looking my plate over. "You're not afraid to eat in front of muthafuckas, that's for sure. Where the fuck do you pack all that food you eat? Oh, wait, never mind, you're sitting on it!" Antwan tilted his head, looking at my booty plopped in the chair across from him.

I rolled my eyes, crossing my legs. "Boy, bye. I'm hungry." I grabbed my fork and started to dig into my plate when Antwan grabbed my hand. I looked up at him.

"Yo, we gotta pray first, shawty." Antwan shook his head at me, looking at me like I was some kind of heathen.

"Oh. Okay." I was shocked a little.

"What, you thought that just because I rap about killing muthafuckas that I don't believe in God?" Antwan asked, eyes searching my face.

"I didn't say that. I just didn't take you as someone who was religious." I watched Antwan laughing a little.

"Yah know, I wear these got-damn braces because I was shot in my jaw at the age of fourteen after my first concert. Niggas from the hood showed up to my concert and shot the place up. They were some niggas that my mother made sure were put away after they broke in her house after finding out that she was my mother. These niggas shot three of my bodyguards and then got to me, shooting me in my jaw three muthafuckin' times. I'm not even supposed to be alive, shawty. I'm not even supposed to be alive to tell you this story. I woke up from a medically induced coma after three days. I was alive. Mouth wired shut. My jaw pops out of place sometimes. I have about five porcelain implants in my mouth. I'll probably have to wear braces until I'm thirty-five, but I'm straight." Antwan grinned. "But ever since the day I got shot, I've been thanking God for every good thing in my life. He brought me through some tough times. Nah, I don't go to church on Sundays, but I pray to God every day that I'm above ground. And you should too."

I gasped a little as Antwan grabbed my other hand, holding it in his. My mouth dropped open a little as I watched him close his eyes.

"God, I thank you… for Audrey." Antwan opened his eyes, looking into mine.

My heart stampeded in my chest. It was the first time that I'd ever heard anyone other than Mariah say that they were thankful for me. It felt amazing, I must admit, to hear a superstar say they were glad to have me around.

"Amen." Antwan grinned, eyes searching mine.

"A- Amen." I stuttered, glancing over at Mariah, who was giggling with the rest of the crew, who sat watching my face turning bright red.

"Sean, who?" Drizzle smirked, sitting across from Rhandy at the booth across the room from ours.

I sighed as I slid my hands from Antwan's. "So, you're from Florida too, huh?"

Antwan nodded, starting to dig into his food. "Tallahassee. That's where my family is from. We lived there until I was about four and Grandma moved to Severn. We've been back and forth between Maryland and Florida until I got my record deal in high school. Did my accent give me away?"

I hesitated. "No. Your mother was visiting family members in Jacksonville when she was in that car accident. If she hadn't have been there, I wouldn't be here."

Antwan looked at me before putting a spoonful of mashed potatoes in his mouth.

"I have dreams about her holding you and your brother in the hospital. Crying to her mother, telling them that she was afraid she wouldn't treat the two of you fairly because of what your father did to her." I had to tell Antwan. "I think she loved you. I think there was more going on that the two of you don't know about. In my dreams, she kept a diary. I think she has a storage somewhere."

Antwan's eyebrows knitted together.

"You know," I laughed a little. "Before the accident, I didn't wear glasses. And now I do. Your mother wore glasses. Chanel glasses, to be exact. I remember that from when she made appearances to our school growing up."

"So, how did you meet that nigga, Sean?" Antwan changed the subject.

I looked at him, picking up my big-ass crispy piece of fried chicken. "Oh, we grew up together. Our parents were close friends. We grew up next door to each other when I lived in the Provinces. Went to school together until we moved to Columbia. We all grew up together. Me, Mariah, Sean, Brandie's dumb-ass, Korey…"

Antwan looked up at me. "Korey? Your manager?"

I nodded. "Yes. He had the biggest crush on me. He couldn't figure out for the life of me why I was fuckin' with Sean. Sean wasn't always this way."

Antwan scoffed. "The hell he wasn't. He's been that way for the entire six years that I've known him, shawty. I knew him a few years before he signed with Ervin. He was always that same, sneaky, grimy muthafucka. He was always fuckin' someone else's girl. I guess I didn't have a problem with that shit until he started fuckin' with mine."

I looked at Antwan. "So, is that why you signed me? Just to spite him?"

Antwan looked at me. "Is that why you signed with me? Just to spite the muthafucka too?"

I just looked at Antwan.

"I found out you were the one writing Sean's songs. He slipped up and told one of the dancers. Laurie, the same dancer who left us and went to A.J. Miller. And A.J. Miller wanted to work with Sean just to get to you too. You hit the club, Club Onyx in Towson, a few months ago with your girls, and I saw you out there on the dance floor. One of my dancers pointed you out. I was like, shawty is cute as a muthafucka. I couldn't let you get caught up in that shit with your boy and A.J. Miller. I told Karen that when I came home after my tour, that I wanted to have a contest at my brutha's club. I was hoping the crowd would pick you, but regardless, I had already chosen." Antwan watched me take a huge bite out of that big ass chicken thigh.

I looked at him, not saying a word until I chewed the food that was in my mouth. "So, you call yourself rescuing me. Is that it?"

126

THE LYRICS TO HIS SONG

Antwan shook his head a little. "I can't save anyone who doesn't wanna be saved, shawty. Karen told me that she wants to sign you as her singer, and Sean told the entire tri-state area that you accepted his proposal. Looks to me like you got everything all figured out. That you don't need my help. I could be wrong, but I think you actually think that that got-damn paper from the magistrate's office is gonna change that nigga. That changing your last name to Lee is going to make him love you that way that you love him. I don't understand how niggas like him get the good girls, and the loyal niggas like me get the gold diggin', sleep-with-your-entire-squad, dick-hoppin' bitches. Why don't girls like you fall for guys like me?"

Oh, I wanted to fall for someone like Antwan, but fuckin' with him seemed like a lot of trouble. And he was right. The more I thought about having lunch with my family, the more I thought about what I was going to say to my family about my proposal. If I knew Sean, he was going to propose to me over lunch, in front of our parents, ya know, for shock-and-awe affect. He was going to slide that ring onto my finger in front of my father, the man who wanted to see his daughter get married. In front of my mother, who wanted me to end up with a man who could take care of me. And in front of his mother, who told him he'd never amount to anything, that he would end up in jail, just like his father, or dead, just like his brother, Johnny, who was shot by the police when we were just twelve-years old. We both had lost a sibling that was close to us; we both understood the loss of a loved one. Before Sean had the music, he had me. Once he got his time to shine, he didn't need me anymore. He forgot that I needed him though.

"The muthafucka was high out of his mind when I saw him at that party last night. I don't know what the muthafucka took, but I saw him drinking some shit, smoking some shit, poppin' some pills, and snorting some shit up his nose at my brutha's club before the talent show yesterday." Antwan shook his head. "But no amount of being high would make me smack the shit out of you. That's what he did, right? You have fingerprints around your neck, too, like the nigga was holding you down by your neck or something. The nigga did more than smack you, didn't he?" Antwan watched me not able to look at him. "A'ight, you wanna keep what he did a secret, then go ahead. It's probably best that you don't let a nigga know. Lyric, don't marry this nigga. I promise, if you walk down the aisle with that clown, I'm gonna clown. You're not my girl, nah, but you sure as hell have no business being his. I'ma act a fool on your wedding day so you might as well make sure I don't find out the date, time, or place of that shit. Believe that. On my word, I'm gonna kill that muthafucka and any muthafucka who agrees with you marrying that muthafucka."

"Damn right!" Mariah cosigned from across the room.

I shot her a quick glare before looking back at Antwan. "I appreciate your concern, but I can look out for myself."

"But you're not by yourself. I got you." Antwan whispered

I sighed.

"You're the lyrics to my song, Audrey, not his. Remember that." Antwan reminded me.

I just looked at him, not really sure what to say. And not really sure what I'd allowed my heart to get involved with. I'd only known the dude for two days, but it was obvious that we'd connected. I wasn't sure if it was his mother's heart that led me to her son or if I was just drawn to him because I wasn't supposed to be. Regardless, I sat there with Antwan for hours, talking to him like we were old friends catching up. It was funny because there were a lot of memories that Antwan told me that felt like deja-vu. Like I'd experienced those exact same experiences that he did or like I was there when his experiences happened. For instance, he mentioned having a baby with Brenda when he was just thirteen years old. I remember going to the neonatal intensive care unit at Johns Hopkins Hospital where Antwan said the baby was born. I remember asking about the little girl's condition. She was a tiny frail little baby, couldn't have been more than three pounds, if that. When Antwan mentioned that the baby died in Brenda's arms when she was just three days old, I remember watching the two crying and wailing over the baby, watching them from a distance, holding the baby in the ICU. I even remember sitting in the audience at Antwan's high school graduation. I remember how loud the screams were coming from the crowd of family members, school faculty, and his fellow graduates. Strangely enough, I even remember the lullaby that Antwan's grandmother used to sing to him to put him to sleep as a child. His mother must have gone to see her boys on occasion; there's no way I would have had the visions of her children the way that I did.

After talking for about an hour and a half, everyone was ready to leave. All but Antwan, and myself, I hate to admit. Antwan told the others to go on without us. So, three bodyguards stayed behind with us, and everyone else left. I wasn't sure what to think. I was so not ready to talk to Antwan on my own. He was a little too bold and assertive for me. The more I tried to deny my attraction, the more he did to draw me back in. It felt so nice to actually spend time with someone who thought about my needs and wants for a change. He asked me where I wanted to go since we were in D.C. I said I wanted to just walk along the National Harbor. It wasn't too windy that day to take a walk outside. As a matter-of-fact, the sun shone bright in the sky that day. I needed some air before my birthday lunch with my family. The family I barely saw. The last time I had lunch with my family was the day of my little sister, Amber's graduation, the Spring before. Almost a year without visiting home. I lived in Hanover, probably twenty minutes from my parents, and I never went home. I wasn't looking forward to their lectures or of my mother ogling over Sean when she didn't know shit about him. Even after all my mother had gone through with my father, that woman was still in love with the idea of being in love.

"I can't believe you are sipping on that cold ass smoothie in February, shawty!" Antwan laughed at me as we walked along the sidewalk of the National Harbor.

I made a face at him. "What do you mean? This strawberry smoothie is giving me life!"

Antwan grinned, snatching the cup from me, placing the straw to his lips and sipping from it. The look on his face though when he tasted how good and soothing it was.

I blushed a little. "See. It's good, right?"

"It's good, but I'm trying to taste what your mama made." Antwan licked his lips as he handed the cup back to me.

I was confused. "What's that?"

"You." Antwan grinned, watching my eyes widen. "You weren't ready for that one, huh?"

I shook my head at him. "You are really something else, Antwan." I sipped from my smoothie. "So cocky."

"Cocky fresh, huh?" Antwan pulled his baseball cap down over his head a little.

I liked the sound of that. "I could write a song about how 'cocky fresh' you are, Antwan." I looked at his baseball cap. "So, what's with this label you and your brother came up with? I see everyone rockin' it. People go broke for this shit. I have friends who won't even pay their bills just so they can get the clothes and the shoes as soon as they drop, Antwan!"

Antwan grinned. "That's wild. I wouldn't go broke for no muthafucka. The point of this clothing line was to show everyone that just because you're from the ghetto doesn't mean you can't overcome. Doesn't mean you can grow. Doesn't mean you can't make it. We made it. I left the hood. Apollo is rich like a muthafucka. He rides around in a damn old ass Cutlass, while he has his girl riding around in a got-damn Benz. The only reason he doesn't wanna leave the hood because his girl won't leave. He's been fuckin' with ol' girl since like the third grade, man."

I shrugged. "That's good, right?"

"Nah, that's stupid." Antwan scoffed. "Yeah, me and my brutha are always foolish when it comes to love. We pick that one girl and stick with her."

I rolled my eyes, remembering all the stories that I would overhear Brandie and her girls talking about when they'd come to Foot Locker just to stand around, boasting about the shit.

"Well, that's not what I heard. You hoe."

132

Antwan shook his head. "Eh, when I'm single, I'm single; I do what the fuck I want. But when I find someone, I stick with her. It's just me and her. I was in love with Brenda. I would have done anything for her. Was no way in hell I'd ever cheat on her. I was loyal as a muthafucka. You know how it is, Ma." Antwan nudged me. "When you only want one person, everyone else is whack as fuck."

I nodded, thinking about how much in love I was with Sean's ole stupid ass. "True. Wish it wasn't that way, but it is."

Antwan looked at me. "We need to get back to the parking lot where my bodyguards are parked. I got a lot to do today. Maybe I should get you back to the crib." Antwan watched the disappointed look on my face, and I think he was actually happy to see it. He grinned a little. "I wasn't doing shit but planning for my meeting with my publicist and a few investors about some ideas I have. What are you getting into this afternoon? You got plans?"

I hesitated. "Not really. I just wasn't trying to go home or hang with Mariah. I already know she's about to drill me about what went down with Sean last night. Not really trying to get into it with her either. It's over and done. The muthafucka doesn't even remember what he did to me. In his eyes, it's like the shit never even happened."

I loved the sympathetic look on Antwan's face. I didn't get that look from any men in my life too often. I cherished the moments when men gave a fuck about me. The moments were brief and rare.

I sighed, watching Antwan's eyes dance from mole to mole on my face. I shied my gaze away for a few seconds before looking back up at him. "I'm just about to go home, get in the bed, pop open a bottle of Moscato, and watch Waiting to Exhale."

Antwan laughed a little. "Waiting to...? Nah. Roll with me to my condo in Bethesda."

I shook my head frantically. Wasn't no way in hell that I was going anywhere alone with that boy. The only boy I'd ever been alone with was Sean. Antwan was like Sean in no way, but he was a man. A man who made it perfectly clear in front of his crew that he was going to get me at any cost.

"I don't know, Antwan." I sipped from my cup.

"It's cool. It's my home away from home. Not sure I wanna take you to my mansion. Too many paparazzi like to hang outside of my crib. I wanna take you somewhere quiet. No one knows where this place is but my bodyguards. Nobody who can afford to live in the building knows anything about me or listens to hip-hop. I go there when I just need to get away from everyone. You seem like you need to get away from everyone for a while." Antwan looked down into my face as we stopped walking.

I just looked at him.

THE LYRICS TO HIS SONG

"Come on, shawty. We didn't really get in any work today. We can write music together. You can trust me, Lyric. I just wanna know you. I think we have a lot to talk about. Shit, a lot to write about. Let's go vent on paper." Antwan grabbed my hand.

So, I rode in the backseat of Antwan's limo to his place. I sat next to him, dozing off, head on his shoulder. I don't know why I was so comfortable with him when I should have shied away from him. My cell phone must have vibrated in my pocket twenty times on my way to Antwan's place. And I didn't have to look at the display to see that it was either Mariah, Sean, or my mother. I just wanted to get away from stress for a few hours. And apparently, so did Antwan. We stepped out of his ride that afternoon, standing in front of twelve story tall Lionsgate Condominiums. Antwan was right; just about everyone who passed us on the way into the building, and as we walked our way through the lobby of the building, looked like people who were too high in status to listen to hip-hop. We didn't get any awkward stares and were greeted politely. I guess though they didn't know anything about Antwan Jared, they knew the dude had to be somebody who was making bank to live in a place like that and to have three bodyguards surrounding him.

I was in awe as I walked through the building. "This place is... wow!" I clenched his forearm tightly with both hands as I ogled over the glistening lobby, watching the attentive staff great Antwan with a smile.

Antwan and his bodyguards laughed at me.

When I stepped onto the gleaming hardwood floors of Antwan's condo, I thought I had died and gone on to heaven. The place was spectacular. Luxurious living room decorated with the latest gray luxury modern furniture. Gourmet kitchen with granite countertops. Stainless steel appliances. As clean as that place was, I knew that boy had a maid or almost never came to the place. There wasn't a speck of dust or fingerprint on anything. And the view from the eighth floor was magnificent. But what caught my eye was the piano that sat in the corner of the living room.

Antwan stood in the doorway of his place, talking to his bodyguards, eying me as I walked towards the piano. "Eh, Gavino, y'all can roll out, get something to eat or whatever. Me and shawty are good." He dapped the tall bodyguard.

"You sure?" Gavino asked, "A'ight, well, ya know I live about fifteen minutes away, son. You need us, we're only a call away. As a matter-of-fact, once we get something to eat, we'll take turns parking outside of the building, a'ight? Too much crazy shit going on to leave you alone for too long, boss man."

I played a few notes on the ivory keys of the piano. I'd seen that piano before, or at least felt like I'd seen one similar. I sat down at the wooden bench, closing my eyes for a few seconds. In my head, I saw a little girl sitting next to a woman in a white dress. The little girl rested her hands on top of the woman's hands as the woman played music composed by Chopin.

Antwan cleared his throat as he closed the front door to his condo. "My mother did have a storage unit, shawty. When she died, they auctioned off everything. She was married to that nigga, Judge Troy Michael. A few days after my mother's funeral, this nigga shows up to my mansion with this piano, saying my mother would've wanted me to have it. That …"

I looked at Antwan as he walked up to me.

"That she said if anything were to happen to her, to make sure that I got this piano." Antwan sat down beside me, taking off his baseball cap, sitting it on top of the piano. "Judge Michael said my mother would stay up all hours of the night writing music. She even wrote songs about me and Apollo." Antwan reached for a notebook that sat on top of the piano. And he handed it to me.

I opened it, flipping the page to a song she composed called A Song for my Sons. I glanced at Antwan before flipping to the next page. And the next. And then the next. The entire notebook was filled with music and lyrics for her sons. And I knew those songs. I flipped to a page with a son called 'A Lullaby for Antwan', the same song I remember his grandmother singing to him. She did, in fact, miss her boys. She did, in fact, love them. There were reasons why she gave her sons up. More to it than not being able to love them because she was raped.

I looked at Antwan. "Has anyone else seen this?"

Antwan shook his head. "Nah. I haven't even showed Apollo." He placed his hands on the ebony and ivory keys of the piano and played the most beautiful song. "This song is my favorite. It's called, Taken From My Arms." Antwan played the song for about two minutes before the pain set in his soul, and he couldn't play anymore.

I eyed Antwan's profile as he sat there, shaking his head to himself, his eyebrows knitting together, his temples twitching. I watched as he slipped his hands from the piano. And I placed my hands on the keys, somehow continuing the song without even eying the sheet music that she'd composed. I was playing the song from what seemed like memory.

Antwan looked at me, his eyes glistening. He watched me playing the song in its entirety. A song that I never even knew that I knew. Shit, I'd never played an instrument in my life, and there I was, playing the piano as if I'd paid thousands for lessons. And I began humming the melody to the song. There were words to the song, and I knew the lyrics.

"I loved you both at first glance; you were so small, you fit in my hands. One had eyes the color of honey; the other's eyes were as green as money." I glanced at Antwan as tears slid down his face.

THE LYRICS TO HIS SONG

"I held you close, kissed you both; it hurt to hear you cry. I hope you both remember me; I never wanted to leave your side. Oh, you boys were a sight to see. I didn't leave you; they took you from me..." I stopped singing the song, my heart slamming against my ribcage, sharp pain in my chest. The memories were painful, literally for the both of us.

Antwan dried his face, watching me rubbing my chest. "You a'ight?"

I looked at Antwan. He did have eyes the color of honey. I grinned a little, slightly freaked out that I knew the lyrics and melody to a song that I'd never heard, yet somewhat satisfied knowing that his mother thought about her boys enough to compose an entire notebook worth of songs about them. "She loved you both, Antwan."

"Yeah? Then why did she leave us?" Antwan disagreed.

"I don't think she left you. You said you were from Florida, but the papers always said your mother was from Connecticut. How did your mother even get caught up with A.J. Miller? The grandma that passed away, was that her mother? Or A.J. Miller's?" I threw a couple of questions at Antwan.

Antwan shrugged. "I don't know the answer to any of those questions, shawty. All I know is we ended up in the hood, being raised by muthafuckas who could care less if we ate, bathed, or went to school. Queen's own father was raping her. Do you know how many times she ran away, only to be brought right back to the muthafucka? Do you know me and Apollo killed that nigga—our own uncle—when we were seventeen when we found out that he'd gotten Queen pregnant? Queen was living with her friend, Lacy Rodgers, then. Uncle Walter broke in one night when Lacy was at work and raped my cousin. Queen was nineteen."

My eyes grew big.

Antwan nodded. "Yeah, man, my cousin gave birth to a dead baby when she was just seven months pregnant. The baby was dead inside of her. They made Cuz push her dead baby girl out of her. I guess God knew my cousin couldn't live with that pain. And we couldn't either. Killed that muthafucka. I can't tell you whose side of the family raised us because no one's last name was Miller or Jared. Grandma never married and wouldn't talk about my mother or about A.J. All I know is my life sucked until I met Ervin and Karen. I thought they were my family until they started thinking A.J. was the solution to all of their money problems. I have a feeling shit is going to get real ugly real fast. My contract with Instinctive isn't up for another two years. So, even though I'm starting my own label, I'm still bound by law to the Blacks. But you're not. So, whatever music you write is yours, not theirs. They get no penny for anything that you write for me. You got it? Nobody owns your lyrics but you."

"I don't have to sing anything, do I? I'm so not a singer." I sighed.

"Then what was that you just did a few minutes ago? What was that you did on stage last night?" Antwan's eyes searched my face.

I shrugged. "A few minutes ago? That was your mama singing. And last night, shit, that was anger singing. Now, if you want me to write music, I can do that, but as far as singing goes, the only thing you'll get out of me is singing hooks, in the background, not center stage. Last night was a once in a lifetime thing."

Antwan grinned. "I can sing."

"What?" I looked into his face, watching him laugh. "Boy, bye. I've never heard you sing one bit in any of your music, and I've been listening to your shit since you and Apollo were posting videos on You Tube."

"What will it take to get you center stage again? Will I have to sing wit'cha? Is that what it's gonna take?" Antwan's eyes searched mine. Antwan's fingers began stroking the keys to the melody of Usher's Nice and Slow.

I grinned, looking down at his fingers before looking back into his face.

"It's seven o'clock, on the dot, I'm in my drop top, cruising the streets. Oh, yeah…" Antwan grinned, watching me cheesing.

I squealed, clapping my hands together. "Oh my God!" I squealed before laying my head on that boy's shoulder. My heart melted in my chest. The sound of that boy's voice was music to my soul. That boy's voice grabbed ahold of my soul and wouldn't let go. I listened to him singing the first verse of one of my favorite songs. The song brought back bittersweet memories, but I tried focusing on Antwan and that phenomenal, strong voice of his. Sean was dating this chick named Monique back in high school, but when he asked me to go with him to see Usher in concert, I didn't hesitate. Usher was serenading the crowd with that song when Sean and I had our first kiss. I was fifteen years old and in love with a boy who was loved by all the hoes. I was so stupid. And apparently much hadn't changed. I was about to be even stupider and let my family talk me into marrying that boy.

I lifted my head from Antwan's shoulder, looking his face over as he sang.

"Let me take you to a place that's nice and quiet, where there ain't no one there to interrupt. Ain't gotta rush. I just wanna take it nice and slow…" He closed his version of the song.

"Wow," was all I could say. I just looked at Antwan, watching him exhale deeply. "Why don't you ever sing? The girls would go crazy over that shit! Shit, feel this!" I grabbed Antwan's hand, placing it on my chest, over my heart.

Antwan grinned, eyes searching my face.

"You have my heart racing, Antwan! You feel that shit?" I exhaled deeply, watching Antwan's smile fade as he watched my chest heave in and out. "What's wrong?" I asked him.

"This is the first time I've ever felt my mother's heartbeat, Lyric… This moment is real intense right now." Antwan shook his head to himself before slipping his hand from under mine.

"And I ain't trying to be one of them sing-your-girl-a-love-song type nigga, Lyric. I'm a rapper. Straight thug-music 'til the day I die. The girls gone always want the Jeweler. You'll wish you came to Jared, too, once you realize what a mistake you made fuckin' around with Sean's weak ass."

I rolled my eyes, though I was in total agreement with his cocky ass.

I watched him get up from the stool.

"Yo, you wanna go up on the terrace? They serve cocktails up there in about," Antwan looked at his watch, "twenty minutes."

We went out to the terrace that afternoon, drinking with the other tenants who were upstairs, enjoying the view as well. I must admit, it was nice talking to people who weren't so ratchet for a change. They asked about the two of us and how we met, and of course, Antwan told them the story of how my life was saved because of his mother's car accident. They swore up and down that meeting each other was in our destiny. We talked to one of the older couples who lived a few condos down the hallway from him. Mr. and Mrs. Starr was the couple's name. Mr. Starr told us how he never knew his mother either. A few years ago, Mr. Starr received a liver transplant. He told us how he started having memories of a man's childhood. Mr. Starr researched his donor's history and turned out that man was his brother. Turned out, his mother was alive and living in a nursing home. She had her son when she was young and gave him up for adoption. When she tried to get him back a few years later, the family disappeared, changing their last name. The story was amazing. Though Antwan tried to hide his emotions, I knew he felt like meeting me was going to lead to him finding out more about why his mother really gave him up.

I stayed with Antwan the entire day. We ate dinner at Black's Bar and Kitchen on Woodmont Avenue. The bodyguards showed up, staying within close proximity, but had changed into casual attire so that they wouldn't be so obvious. I had a great time with Antwan that day. I saw a side of that boy that I didn't see on television. He wasn't a thug or a nigga with street credibility. He was just Antwan Jared, a boy who needed some air from the fame for a while. We sat poolside that night. I think we must have written about ten songs that night. My favorite song was the one that I'd freestyled the first few lines to in the studio for him, The Difference Between You and Me. We finished it together, adding three more verses. Adding a catchy hook. All we needed was Drizzle to give us that beat. And we had ourselves a hit for sure.

"Oh my goodness." I looked at my Adidas watch. "It's already 12:30 in the morning?"

"Shit, I guess time flies when you're having fun, huh?" Antwan watched me closing my lyrical journal.

I still hadn't touched that iPad that Karen had given me earlier that day. I liked doing things the old fashioned way. Fuck that technical shit. I liked scribbling in my pad. It was my baby. I took that leather notebook everywhere.

I looked at Antwan. "I had a great time today. I haven't had this much fun in—"

Antwan cut me off. "Let's be real. You've never had this much fun, huh?"

I looked at him.

He looked at me.

We both chuckled a little.

"Shut up, Antwan. Sheesh. No, okay?" I rolled my eyes, trying not to grin at him and his shiny-ass braces.

"You might as well just stay here tonight. No use going back home this time of night. Your nigga's not home anyway. My mans and them texted me earlier, telling me that they saw the nigga at Columbia Mall with his moms and shit. Yo, his mama's a bitch." Antwan shook his head.

"You don't even have to tell me, Antwan. She's always treated Sean like shit. Johnny was always her favorite. Ever since he was killed, she's been super hard on Sean. Has always made him feel worthless. I try building him up, but you already see how that goes. He's always running from me." I sighed, crossing my legs, leaning back in my seat.

"Well, let him run then, shit." Antwan scoffed. "We all have problems. The shit he's been through with his family has nothing to do with what he's been through with you. Up until yesterday, I didn't even know Sean had a girl. And that's fucked up. He's been fuckin' around with your girl, Fatima, too."

I widened my eyes, sitting back up in the chair. "You knew?"

Antwan scoffed. "Shit, everybody but Snare knows that shit. I caught the two fuckin' a few months ago. I don't even think Fatima's son is Snare's. He looks just like your nigga, shawty. But judging by the look on your face, you already knew that." Antwan shook his head at me, probably thinking I was pathetic as a muthafucka.

"Karen told me today in her office. I didn't wanna call him out in front of Snare, but yeah, I know about it." I sighed.

"You're a good one, shawty. Cuz I'm ready to whip ya nigga for you for that shit. Fatima ain't ya girl neither." Antwan had to remind me.

"And the worse part about it all is that Fatima is like family. I'm sure my family will invite her to lunch tomorrow since Sean let everybody know that he's proposing to me. I already know my mom is going to invite her. Not looking forward to this one bit." I exhaled deeply.

"Then don't go. The nigga wants to ask your parents for your 'hand in marriage' after the fact? After he already announced on the radio that you'd already said yes to the nigga? After he's had two babies on you? After he put his muthafuckin' hands on you? After he had you busting your ass at Foot Locker and shit, while he's going broke for Fatima, Brandie, and the rest of them bitches?" Antwan frowned. "You can't be this stupid, Lyric, or this desperate."

I resented that, though it wasn't like the dude was lying. "What is that supposed to mean, Antwan?"

"Just what I said." Antwan wasn't backing down. "You talked all that shit on stage to the nigga, and then you went back to the nigga that night. That's the type of nigga you think you deserve? The type of nigga that doesn't give a fuck about you, except for when it's convenient for him? He wasn't paying you any mind until he thought I was tryin' to snatch ya ass up."

I looked at Antwan. "I'm really not trying to hear this shit, Antwan."

"The nigga is fuckin' with one of your best friends, has a got damn two-year-old son with that bitch! And the nigga has a three-year-old baby with another chick—" Antwan started to go in on me about my stupidity, but I cut him off.

"Your chick?" I rolled my neck at him.

Antwan made a face. "The fuck? 'My chick'? You think I give a fuck about Brenda? She made her bed, she's gotta lie in that bitch. Karma's fuckin' her world up; she's the least of my concern. My concern is you, shawty."

"Me? Looks to me like you're trying to run my life like everyone else is doing. All I wanted to do was prove to Sean that my life matters too. I wasn't trying to get caught up with anything that's going on between the two of you! You're using me to get to him, he's using me to get to you, and I'm not about to get stuck in the middle!" I got up from the table that we sat at.

"All I am to you are the lyrics to your song. You remember that, Antwan!"

"Nah, you're more than that." Antwan got up from the table, catching my arm before I stormed off from him.

"Two days, Antwan. That's how long you've known me. I've known Sean for two fuckin' decades!" I pulled from him.

Antwan took a deep breath, trying his best to choose his words carefully. "I just don't understand how you can love a nigga like that nigga. You've known this nigga all your life—and, so fuckin' what? I bet he's been fuckin' your heart up your entire life too. I heard you lost his baby in a car accident. That Brenda's baby was born on the same day that your baby was supposed to be born. You can't stand there and tell me that I'm wrong."

My heart slammed against my chest. "You don't have to understand why I'm with him. It's not up to you to decide who I decide to spend my life with. Let's just keep this strictly business, Antwan. Stay in your lane, dude. You stay out of my business, and I'll stay out of yours." I pushed him in his chest.

Antwan looked me over a little before looking into my face. He scoffed. "Well, fuck you, too, then. You want a part-time, fuck-your-friends-and-have-your-ass-babysitting-her-kids muthafucka, then do you, shawty. Y'all women kill me. Y'all diss the good niggas for drug-addicted, manipulative, bitch-ass niggas like that!"

Antwan was really pissed at me.

I broke down and cried, something I wasn't even trying to do in front of someone who was basically a stranger.

Antwan could care less at that point that I was crying. "I was just trying to show you the difference between a nigga like him and a nigga like me. I'm here with you tonight when I could be out there with all these bitches!" Antwan took his phone out of his pocket, showing me all his notifications, texts, inbox messages, missed calls, and voicemail messages.

I looked into his face, drying my face as his phone started vibrating again. I looked down at the display, the initials "QF3" flashing across the display.

Antwan looked at his display and then back into my face. "Quick Fuck #3. I don't even know shawty's name. All I know is she calls me whenever her man is out of town or whenever she wants to pop a couple bottles with me and my niggas. Shit, QF2 is gonna call in about fifteen minutes." His phone vibrated again. He looked at the display. "Oh, here goes HG4. Head Game #4. Haven't heard from her in a minute." He opened up the text that she sent "Hey, boo. I'm in town. Hit me back. Can't wait to suck your dick.' Oh, and she attached a picture of her suckin' her nigga's dick. You wanna see."

Oh, Antwan pissed me the fuck off. I didn't even know why I was so mad. He could have been with anyone that he wanted, but he was there with me. And all I could think about was the look on my parents' face when they saw Sean slide that expensive ass diamond ring onto my finger.

Before Antwan could show me the picture that one of his jump offs sent to him, I slung that fuckin' iPhone into the pool. Antwan looked at me like I was crazy.

"Go get it," he scoffed.

"Hell nah, nigga." I rolled my neck and folded my arms.

My phone rung in my pocket.

Antwan looked into my face before grabbing my body to his by my hips.

I gasped as this fool dug through my pockets for my old beat up ass Samsung Galaxy with the cracked screen. I tried to snatch the phone from him as he looked at the display.

"It's ya nigga. Want me to answer it, telling him you've got a dick in you? I bet the nigga will straighten up then." Antwan acted like he was about to press 'talk' on the phone.

"Antwan, you better not!" I squealed just as he tossed the phone over my head and into the pool.

I pushed Antwan in his chest. "Antwan! I've had that phone for four fuckin' years! That was my brother's phone! Go get it! I'm sorry that I threw your phone in there, but please, get my brother's phone!" I turned around, eyes searching the water for the phone. I was damn near on my tiptoes. And just when I spotted the phone, I lost my balance.

Antwan caught me but lost his balance, too, and there we were, in that cold-ass swimming pool. I came up for air, pushing my bushy hair from my face. I squealed, swiping the water from my face. Antwan didn't come up for air with me. There he was, swimming to the bottom of the pool for both of our phones. I grabbed his hat that was floating in the water. Then, I watched as Antwan swam his way back up to me. He swiped the water from his face. Do you know that muthafucka's phone was still vibrating off the hook? Meanwhile, my phone's screen was black, casing full of water. I snatched the phone from him before swimming the short distance back to the edge of the pool.

"You're welcome." Antwan laughed a little, swimming behind me.

Antwan helped me out of the pool before climbing out behind me.

I squealed as the wind blew through my wet clothes. "I could kill you, Antwan!" I shivered before Antwan surrounded me in his arms. I swear on my life, I'd never gotten a hug so tight, so strong, so embracing. I sighed, heart trembling in my chest. "Oh my goodness," I muttered to myself, wrapping my arms around him too. "As wet as we both are, this feels so fuckin' good."

Antwan laughed, heart beating against mine. "Let's go change, shawty."

So, of course my dumb ass didn't stay the night with Antwan. We went inside and got out of those wet clothes. Of course, I had to wear something from his closet. T-shirt, tank top, boxers, socks, sweats, and Nike sandals.

Antwan laughed at me as I dried my hair with a towel, coming out of his bathroom.

"I look like a hood nigga for real in these baggy clothes, Antwan." I rolled my eyes at him, eying my phone drying out on his bookshelf as I passed it in the hallway.

"Hey, you're the one that started this shit." Antwan grinned at me, dressed in all black, looking like he was about to hit the club since I told him there was no way in hell that I was spending the night. "I'm sorry about your phone, shawty. You backed up your numbers, right?"

"Hmph." I ignored him, towel drying my hair, eying his attire.

"Where are you going?"

"My brother just hit me up. I'ma drop you off and then roll out." Antwan watched me roll my eyes.

"Trying to hook up with Desperate Dick Sucking Bitch #3, huh?" I watched Antwan burst out laughing. "I think that Head Game chick just texted you back."

Antwan smacked his lips. "Ain't nobody trying to be shawty's side nigga. I don't even know her name. All I know is she has no problem putting dick in her mouth. It's been months since I fucked around with her." He looked me over, watching me adjust the drawstring on his pants. "You're looking real cute in my sweats, ol' midget-ass."

I rolled my eyes, attempting to walk past him over to my clothes. He really hurt my feelings when he told me that I must have been desperate to fuck with a nigga like Sean. No, I wasn't desperate. I just needed Sean's love. Or at least I thought I did. I found it really hard to accept Antwan's kindness. I'd never been treated like I was someone's everything before. I'd just met Antwan, and he just seemed too nice. The dude was a muthafuckin' superstar. I heard the stories about him and his crew. It was no secret that he got around. But I saw a different side of Antwan. He'd made me feel ways that Sean never bothered to even acknowledge that I needed to feel. Sean was too comfortable with me. Outside of sex, he treated me like I was one of the homeboys instead of his girl. I needed to be his girl. Maybe a part of me hoped that ring would change how he perceived me.

Antwan caught my arm, pulling me back to him. He caught wind of the attitude that I had towards him for what he had said earlier. "I ain't trying to be your man. All I'm saying is the nigga you're with doesn't love you."

"You told me back in that studio today that you didn't know nothing about love," I reminded him.

"And I don't. Shit, what do you know about love? What does love know about you? Apparently, nothing. Fuck love; love is for dreamers.

Dreamers can have that fake ass shit. My point is," Antwan huffed, "I just couldn't help but notice you weren't being treated right. I don't like seeing a good woman being treated like she ain't a good woman. If you were mine, I'd show you off like you were my brand-new car. Spoil the shit out of you. You deserve that. You know that right?" Antwan pulled the drawstring to his sweats, pulling it as tightly as he could so that it wouldn't fall over my hips. His fingers purposely grazed against my skin as he pulled down the white t-shirt that I was wearing. He shook his head, eying the bruises on my face.

"I never knew loving him would hurt, Antwan." I finally admitted out loud. "But that's my problem, not yours. Now take me home, please."

Antwan's driver drove me back to my place that night, bag full of wet clothes and shoes. Antwan refused to let me walk up to the apartment building by myself. He stood facing me in front of the locked entrance to the building that I lived in.

"Happy Valentine's Day, Lyric." Antwan grinned down at me.

I blushed a little, realizing that it was not only Valentine's Day but my birthday as well.

"Happy Valentine's Day to you too. And it's my birthday."

"Uh-oh, the big two-two." Antwan nudged me. "Happy birthday. See, you should've spent the night. We could have had a slumber party."

I laughed out loud. "Right, Antwan. Anyway, so, I guess I'll see you Monday?"

Antwan shook his head. "Nah, it's your birthday. You gotta let me take you out. Come on." He watched me shake my head hesitatingly. "Just for a drink or something. Not a date but a business meeting. Strictly business, I swear. Thug's honor."

I giggled, pushing him in his chest as he grabbed me close. I looked into his face. I really did have a good time with him, and I wanted to tell him without giving him the impression that we were ever stepping out of the friend zone.

"I'm glad I met you, Lyric." Antwan's eyes traced my lips. "I meant no disrespect to you or your decision to stick by your man. I just wish I had that type of loyalty. I don't want you selling yourself short. Your biggest mistake is thinking that you can change him. Trust me, I know about mistakes. My biggest mistake with the last girl who I claimed as mine was thinking she'd never leave a nigga for another nigga. But she did." Antwan shook his head. "Just be smart about it. You deserve what you've been missing."

"And you think you're gonna be the one to give it to me? You think you're what I've been missing." I shied my gaze away from his, looking down at the ground.

"Damn right I am. I'm yours if you want me. That's my heart beating in your chest. My blood is already running through your veins. It's you and me from this day on out, shawty. You really don't have a choice. I'm here to stay and so are you." Antwan whispered to me.

I sighed as Antwan grabbed me close, giving me that amazing, breathless hug again.

"Why do you have to feel so good?" I said out loud when I meant to make that statement in my head.

Antwan squeezed a little tighter, pressing his lips against my forehead. "Feels good in your arms too." He whispered as I gripped his jacket in my hands. "Audrey, I talked to God about you. I asked him to forgive me."

I looked up at him, my heart going crazy. "Forgive you for what?"

"I asked him to forgive me for lusting after someone else's girl. I told him that I was going to get you by any means necessary, married or not." Antwan's eyes danced over my face, making me feel so hot and bothered.

I had to let him go before my heart got any more caught up in his presence than it already was. "Okay." I laughed nervously, my heart thumping in my chest, the smell of his cologne lingering all over the clothes that he let me borrow. "Ummm, it's late. I need to get inside." I exhaled deeply as Antwan let my body go, only to grab me by the hands instead.

"You didn't think I was gonna let you go without getting a kiss goodnight, did you?" Antwan gently kissed my lips. "Your lip gloss tastes good as a muthafucka…" He nibbled on my bottom lip a little.

I gasped as he kissed my lips again. I swear, his lips were soft as silk. I had never in my life been kissed that way. "Mmmm." I moaned in his mouth as his lips caressed mine. It wasn't until my tongue swiped across his chrome braces that it mentally registered that I was kissing Antwan, and I wasn't supposed to be. By then, it was already too late. Antwan's hands were in my hair. Our lips were already conjoined. My heart was already racing. I think I even heard angels singing, though those may have been the angels that were singing at my funeral when Sean killed us both.

CHAPTER FIVE

Mrs. Lee

"Bless you, boo!" Mariah giggled after making the statement three times the afternoon of Valentine's Day. It was eleven o'clock, and I had just gotten up. I must have gotten three hours of sleep. Once Antwan left that night, all I could think about was that kiss. When I closed my eyes, all I could feel was that boy's lips on mine. I had been kissed by Antwan Jared. It may not have been a big deal to the average twenty-two-year-old, but to me, a girl who was hardly ever kissed, it meant everything.

"Girl." I grabbed a tissue from the box of Kleenex that sat on Mariah's dresser. "I think I'm catching a cold or something. I fell in the pool last night."

Mariah pulled a comb through my natural hair, trying to help me get it situated. "I knew something must have happened. Your hair is nappy-to-be-damned. Girl, I hooked your hair up the other day. Wasted all my got-damn time and you decide you wanna go skinny-dipping with Sean's stupid ass last night." Mariah rolled her eyes.

I sighed. "Did I say anything about Sean? Your ass is always speculating. I haven't seen Sean since he told me that we were having lunch today with our parents." I looked up at Mariah as she slowly pulled the comb through my hair.

Mariah looked down into my face, a slight grin growing across hers. "So... after we left you and 'Twan at Carolina Kitchen, what did y'all do for the rest of the day?"

"Everything." I sighed.

Mariah's eyes widened.

I shook my head frantically before she got the wrong idea. "Not everything."

"Well, you already know how my mind works. My mind lives in the gutter, so you're gonna have to be more specific." Mariah started parting my hair into sections so she could moisturize it before applying heat to it.

"Well, we went to the National Harbor to hang out for a while. We went back to his place. We had a few drinks. We talked. We had interesting conversations with older couples who lived in the building that he lives in. We wrote music. Shit, we came up with this crazy-ass song for the first single on his next album. It's kind of like a rap duet; he's trying to get me to do it with him since it's really a song about the two of us, but I wrote it for Queen to do the vocals. Anyway, we had dinner, and then we wrote some more. Until around 12:30 this morning." I watched Mariah grinning from ear to ear. "What?"

"And?" Mariah wanted me to keep going, as if there was more to tell.

"And what?" I asked.

"You said your ass fell in the pool, Audrey; how the fuck did you end up in the pool? Damn, non-storytelling ass." Mariah shook her head at me.

I rolled my eyes. "Well, he was talking all this shit about how stupid I was for fuckin' with Antwan. Then, the nigga had the nerve to tell me that he could have been with any hoe he wanted; had the audacity to show me all the bitches that were hitting him up on the phone while I was sitting there by that pool on the roof top of that expensive ass building that he lives in. Excuse me, one of the expensive ass buildings that he lives in."

Mariah shrugged with this, 'Shit, he does have a lot of hoes and could have been with all of them at the same time, in front of my ass' look on her face as she started flat-ironing my hair. She was looking at me like I was the one trippin'.

"Well, damn." She cleared her throat. "Was your sister's name poppin' up on his phone?"

I rolled my eyes at her. "All the hoes names were abbreviated. Not one name on the display. The nigga said he didn't even know any of them by name. But he was pissing me off, trying to prove his point of how much he was so-called 'giving up' to spend time with me. So, I tossed his phone in the pool." I watched Mariah's eyes widen before she burst out laughing.

161

"And then my phone started ringing in my pocket."

"Your brother's old cell phone? Oh no…" Mariah shook her head, already knowing what I was about to say.

I nodded. "Yeah. And Sean was calling. And Antwan tossed the shit in the pool. I leaned over the edge of the pool to see if I could spot it. And I lost my balance. Antwan tried catching me and lost his balance, too. We both fell in and—" I sneezed. "Yeah, that's why I'm sneezing."

Mariah laughed a little.

"My phone is fucked up, and his phone is fuckin' waterproof, probably still ringing off the hook." I rolled my eyes. "We changed clothes. He got all dressed up like he was about to go out, which I'm sure he did since I told him I wasn't staying over."

Mariah mushed me in the head. "Idiot!"

I shoved her back.

"You're lucky I don't flat iron your face, Audrey! The fuck?" Mariah scoffed. "You should've stayed your ass with Antwan and said fuck this fake-ass lunch with your family. For real, I'm not even going to do this shit with you, Audrey. I hope the only reason you came to my crib was for me to do your hair. My girl, Breazy, said she only works a half-day today. We're gonna be fuckin' all afternoon, so don't think about poppin' up over here, crying about that nigga because I don't wanna hear shit. I know it's about to be some shit today. I can just feel it!"

I sat back in the chair that I was sitting in, having the same horrible feeling. "Yeah, I can too. But I couldn't stay the night with Antwan. He's just too… too good to be true. He seems like trouble."

"Trouble? Shit, Sean is trouble! He's been trouble since day one. I told you back in school when you were lusting after that nigga that he was no good. He didn't show one bit of real interest in you until you went to prom with that white dude, Billy. Sean didn't want anyone else's dick up in you but his. I'm not stupid. You might have been dazed by the dick, but us rational folks can see right through Sean." Mariah sat the flat iron down on a towel on her dresser before she started brushing the ends of my hair with a round brush.

"Antwan is so different. I don't know if it's because of his mama's heart in my chest that I feel a connection to him or if it's because he shows me attention that Sean doesn't. But whatever the reason, he's right on time." I admitted out loud.

Mariah looked down at me as I looked up at her. She sighed, a sympathetic expression on her face. "I like Antwan for you, but you are right. He is trouble. He is caught up in some crazy shit. I don't want you to get hurt fuckin' with him, but at the same time, Sean ain't shit. And I wanna see Antwan snatch you from this nigga. Just be careful, okay?"

"Antwan kissed me." I sighed.

Mariah just looked at me. She knew how much a kiss meant to me. She knew how much I needed to feel close to someone who I meant everything to. She watched me pout, cry, yell, scream, yearn for Sean's attention, never to really get it. She knew the only reason why I was even considering taking this ring from Sean was because I wanted him to want me. Mariah wanted to smile for me, but she couldn't. She knew I was in trouble.

Mariah shook her head. "You better hope Sean doesn't find out. You already know, based on Antwan's character, he's that in-your-face, yeah-nigga-I-did-it type of nigga. I guarantee you that Antwan's gonna tell your boy he sucked on your face. How much you wanna bet? I bet my lesbianism that this nigga shows out today! I'm not gonna front; Sean goes hard, but Antwan goes harder. I feel sorry for that bastard because he's about to lose you to a real nigga." Mariah watched me roll my eyes. "What? You heard Antwan say he was gonna clown at your wedding! I believe that fool!"

"He doesn't even know me." I sighed, eyeing myself in Mariah's vanity mirror as she slayed my hair.

"That's why I know he's about to act a fool. What dude knows someone for two days and is already this crazy about her?" Mariah smacked her lips. "I told you that someday, someone would care about you the way that you deserved. I told you to wait on him, boo. I told you not to settle for Sean because there would come a day when you wouldn't have to settle. And here Antwan is. Don't go to this lunch. You're gonna regret it."

"Well, you're the one who woke me up this morning. If it hadn't been for you, I would have still been asleep. I just fell asleep at seven this morning. I am not in the mood to see my parents today. You've got something for me to wear to this lunch, right? You know I don't own a skirt or dress of any kind." I sighed.

Mariah dressed me in tight blue polka-dot dress. It was cute in a sixties kind of way. I refused to bust my ass in heels, so I slid into her navy blue pumps from Nine West. Mariah covered my bruises with hypoallergenic make-up by Clinique. She clipped my hair to one side. We both admired my reflection in the mirror. I think Mariah was just as nervous for me as I was for myself.

"I hope the next time I see you that you're not wearing that ring. But good luck anyway, boo. Tell your mom I said kick rocks, okay?" Mariah hugged me around my neck before I walked out of her apartment door.

***

"Audrey! Happy birthday, sis!" My little sister, Amber, hugged me around my neck. I hadn't seen my boo in a minute. She was so petite and short, reminding me of Jada Pinkett when she played in Set If Off. Amber almost never came home. She was a freshman at

Spellman and loving life. She was happy to get away from home. She had no respect for our mother whatsoever. Had no idea how Mama could stay with Father throughout his infidelities. She thought our mother was weak and had no respect for herself or for the two girls that she raised. Alvin hated the way that Dad treated mom. As bad of an example of what a man was supposed to be that my father was, my brother never followed in his footsteps. Alvin respected women. He loved Fatima. And I admit, she was crazy about him. His death fucked her head all the way up. So much that the bitch went to my man for comfort.

"Hey, Amber!" I gave my sister a tight squeeze, meeting her in the foyer of my parents' house. "How have you been?"

"Oh, I'm good." Amber let go of me, looking me over. She grinned, looking up into my face. "Look at my big sista in a tight ass, foxy dress! You look so pretty!"

"Yeah," I rolled my eyes. "Thanks to Mariah. You know she has skills."

"She didn't wanna come to this bullshit either, I see." Amber shook her head at me.

"Everyone's here. Waiting for you in the dining room. You know Sean's bitch ass mama is gonna trip about you being late." Amber took my jacket from my shoulders.

I sighed, walking through the foyer, Amber tossing the white jacket on a coat rack before following behind me. "Who is here?"

"Oh, you'll see." Amber sighed.

I let out a deeper sigh, strolling down the highway. I hesitated before sliding open the door to the dining room. All eyes were on me as I stepped into the room. My mother sat across from Father at the cherry wood dining room table. Ms. Hanna Lee sat across from her son, Sean. Fatima sat to the right of Ms. Lee. And Brandie sat to Sean's right.

Amber made her way around me, going over and sitting at the empty chair left to the of Ms. Lee. And I sighed as Sean got up from his chair to pull the empty chair to his left out so that I could sit in it—something his rude ass had never done. I shook my head at him as I walked over and smoothed my dress out before sitting down in the chair. Sean pushed my chair in before he sat down beside me, looking really handsome in his semi-casual, button down, smoky gray Gucci shirt and black dress pants. I glanced at him before looking at the rest of the house guests.

I looked at my mother as she grabbed my hand.

She gave me an inviting smile before Ms. Lee cleared her throat.

"Audrey, you're late." Ms. Lee rolled her big brown eyes at me, sitting there looking like Claire Huxtable dressed in Jimmy Choo.

I sighed. I seriously hated that bitch. If she wasn't talking shit to her own son about how he was never going to be shit, she was dissing me for fucking with someone like him. "Ms. Lee, thanks for wishing me a happy birthday." I responded sarcastically. "I really appreciate it though it would have been nice to celebrate my birthday separately from lunch with my parents, but thanks. Thank you all." I looked at Fatima, who sat nervously in her chair.

"Well, honey, your boyfriend came to us yesterday morning with some very interesting news." Mother sounded a little too excited about Sean's engagement announcement, as if she'd forgotten all of the things that I'd been through with that fucker over the years.

"Oh, please." Ms. Lee rolled her eyes. Ms. Lee looked at Fatima and then back at me.

"Which news are you talking about? The news about Sean wanting to work with a known drug manufacturer who runs a business where he makes all the money and his artists barely break even? The news about Sean having not one but two children that I'm just now finding out about? The news that neither of these two children are with Audrey, his so-called fiancée? The news that Sean is a drug addict who needs serious help but refuses to acknowledge it? Or the news that these two have no business getting married in the first got-damn place?"

"Whoot!" Amber clapped her hands. "I like her, I'm sorry, Audrey! I think I'm switching teams!"

Ms. Lee looked at Amber and then back at her son. "Don't get me wrong; it's nice to hear that y'all are getting your shit together. It's about time that deejaying is taking you somewhere, even though I don't agree with you working with A.J. Miller. It's about time that you're doing something with your life besides hanging in the streets. You have two mouths to feed. You have not one but two babies with two women, and neither one of them is Audrey, the girl you've known since childhood! Lord have mercy!" Mrs. Lee shook her head, disgusted with her son. Mrs. Lee looked at me. "And you've accepted his behavior all of this time? What does that say about you as a woman? You can't have all that much respect for yourself if you'd allow a man to treat you this way."

My little sister was still cosigning with Ms. Lee. "Amen. At least someone," Amber rolled her eyes at Mother, "recognizes."

Mom rolled her eyes at Amber, still not disagreeing that what Ms. Lee was saying wasn't true.

I sighed. "I had no idea, Mrs. Lee. I just found out yesterday, and he wasn't the one to tell me." I looked over at my father, who sat at the head of the table, fingers intertwined, clearing his throat. He kept quiet, careful not to put his own foot in his mouth. I looked at Fatima, ready to put her ass on blast in front of my family who loved her so much. "Ms. Lee, did Sean tell you that one of his children was with Fatima over here?"

Everyone looked at Fatima and then at Sean before they looked back at me.

Mama stood from the table, her bright skin turning red. "I need to go check on the food." She hurried out of the dining room and into the kitchen.

I watched her leaving me to face the situation alone, as normal. I shook my head, turning to face Sean and Fatima. "All the time, everyone thought you were fuckin' around with Brandie, but it was always Fatima. Wasn't it?"

Brandie turned to Sean, shaking her head at him. "I'm a lot of things, sis, but I'm not one to chase a man who isn't worth chasing. The only thing I ever did for Sean is get my mother to get a few criminal charges dropped, free of charge. Y'all know my mama charges a grip. If it wasn't for me helping him, your boy would have been under the jail, and he knows it. He bought me jewelry from time to time, trying to bribe me into not telling you and Brenda or Fatima. Instead of being worried about me fuckin' with your man, you should've kept your eyes on your so-called friend. Fatima's been in your man's face before our brother passed away, just so you all know."

"Brandie?" Dad finally spoke up. "Let them deal with this situation. A situation that should have been handled way before we had lunch today."

"Oh, you would know about fucked-up situations now wouldn't you, Daddy?" Brandie rolled her eyes at Dad before looking back at Sean.

"He can't do anything to her that she didn't allow." Dad said something that a lot of people didn't realize.

Ms. Lee nodded in agreement. "I told Audrey from jump that she can't trust a man who stays on the road and never takes her. That she can't trust a man who doesn't help pay her bills yet makes six-figures a year. I told her that Sean was either on drugs or he was spending the money on other women, but she never listened to me! He did everything for years to show her that she was the last woman he was thinking about! He only wants her when someone else has their eyes on her! He—"

"He is sitting right here and can talk for himself." Sean cut his mother off, shaking his head at her. "I mean, come on, damn. I am trying to right my wrongs, Mama. I know I did wrong; I know I fucked up."

"It's not only on you; it's on her, too. Because she should have known better." Ms. Lee told me. "You two have no business getting married any time soon. Sean announced on live radio that you two were engaged and that the engagement party is next weekend! This is bullshit! Her own best friend is sitting here, at this dining room table, knowing that she's been sleeping with Sean for years! While she was dating her best friend's brother! She has a two-year-old son with Sean!"

Fatima sighed.

I looked at her. "So, you really have nothing to say in your defense? You've been fuckin' off on not only my brother but with Snare, a nigga who would do anything for you, and you have absolutely nothing to say out'cha mouth, Fatima? Fatima, you were supposed to be one of my best friends! I trusted you!" I stood from the table. Sean tried to grab my arm, but I pulled away from him.

Fatima looked at me, tears in her eyes. "Audrey, I'm sorry."

"Nah, bitch, you're only sorry that you got caught!" I started to go around the table to yank the bitch up by her hair when Brandie jumped up and grabbed me.

I pushed Brandie off of me. "Keep your muthafuckin' hands off of me unless you want some too, Brandie!"

Brandie backed up a little, laughing to herself. "You're taking it out on the wrong people. Sean is the nigga you need to be mad at. She didn't fuck herself, Audrey. This nigga's been drillin' more than Brenda and Fatima. Believe that. I've seen him in action. You're a damn fool if you let him put that ring on your finger, unless you make sure you get this nigga for everything he owns, shit. Don't be stupid, sis!"

Sean stood from the table. "Come on, Ma, sit back down. This isn't how this was supposed to go today."

"Really, Sean?" I turned back around to face him. "Then why the fuck did you let my family invite her? Why is she here? And I don't wanna hear shit about you not fuckin' with this bitch anymore when Mariah said she caught you with the bitch at the after party the other night! What do you have to say about that, huh?"

Sean sighed. "I told you, I don't remember shit that happened the other night. My mom is right; I have a problem. I'm getting help. I start therapy this week. I'm going to check myself into rehab as soon as there's an opening. I swear, I will put in mad overtime to make up for everything that I've done. I can change, Audrey. Please don't walk away from me."

I walked away from Sean midway through his apology speech. I needed to get away from everyone at that table for a few minutes before I completely spazed. My chest was hurting like hell. I went in the bathroom to get a breather. I wasn't there for three minutes when Brandie came barging in on me, closing the door behind her.

"You still don't lock the door when you go in the bathroom, Audrey?" Brandie shook her head at me, leaning back against the door, watching me rubbing my chest. "You need to go get checked out, Audrey. I've been eying you rubbing your chest for about a week now. It's your own fuckin' fault, fuckin' around with this stressful-ass nigga."

I shook my head, waving her off, sitting down on the lid of the toilet. "Brandie, save it, okay? Don't pretend to care about me now. Get out!"

"No, I won't get the fuck out. What the fuck are you doing sitting here in the bathroom? You're the one letting these muthafuckas stress you the fuck out when you have absolutely no reason to be stressed. You finally broke out of that tight-ass shell that you've hidden inside of for years, and it took you thinking your man was fuckin' around with me for you to bust out the muthafucka!" Brandie shook her head at me. "You just signed a phat-ass contract with Antwan Jared! This nigga is about to…" Brandie eyed the way I sighed as soon as Antwan's name came out of my mouth. "Oh," she grinned.

"That's why you're trippin' today."

I looked at her. "What?"

"I saw Antwan at the club around three this morning with his hittas, bitches all in his lap and shit." Brandie grinned at me. "You think that rich nigga wants you? Is that what this is about?"

I shook my head at her shade. "You talk too fuckin' much, Brandie."

"I told you from the day you met Antwan a few years ago and he blew you off that you'd never mean shit to him. All you are to him right now is money. You have dope lyrics; I'll give you that, but it's been war between Sean and Antwan since the day Antwan caught Sean in Brenda's bed. Antwan don't want you; he wants revenge. Confuse revenge with feelings if you want to, sis, and fuck around and get caught up in some bullshit. I'm just trying to tell you. You might as well just stick with Sean if you thinking about Antwan because Antwan's not thinking about you. You can check out Antwan's Facebook page. It's all there for the world to see. Money on money. Hoes on hoes. That's the status he's on. Shit, I hit him up a few times last night, but the nigga didn't answer." Brandie grinned, watching me glare at her.

"Oh, really?" I folded me arms, legs shaking anxiously, wondering if she was Head Game #5 or Deep Throat #2. Lyin' ass nigga. Ugh.

Brandie rolled her eyes at me, "You've loved Sean this long; there's no need to, all of a sudden, start trying to find fault in him now. The nigga could never keep his dick in his pants, and now you wanna get mad? Now you wanna break it off with him? You knew sooner or later someone would get pregnant by the muthafucka! You're lucky all he caught was babies and not STDs! Fuck Fatima. I'd say yes to the nigga just to spite her if I were you. You've always been weak. It's time to be strong. That nigga has never given you shit. You've lost an innocent baby with this muthafucka, only for him to give two other bitches his babies! I say take that ring. Look at this marriage as a business deal. Rumor has it, Sean is about to become partners with A.J. Miller. Not only that, but their company offers incentives to married couples. Whatever he makes in royalties, you get half. When Relentless takes over Instinctive Entertainment, it's a wrap. All those songs that he wrote and produced for Antwan—what, like four albums worth of songs belong to A.J. Miller and Sean Lee once he takes over Instinctive. A third of those songs belong to you, too, if you marry Sean."

I looked at Brandie. Food for thought.

"Take your ass back in the dining room and get'cha ring. Play hard ball wit'cha nigga or something. Shit, grow some balls, Audrey. Stop letting muthafuckas walk all over you. I'm a lot of things, but I'm not a push over. Me and you may not always get along, Audrey, but we're still blood. No matter how we came about being sisters, we're still blood. I'll catch ya later, sis. I have a date. Remember what I said. Let that muthafucka put a ring on it." Brandie sighed before turning back around and leaving the bathroom.

I reluctantly went back into the dining room. Fatima's scary ass was gone. Mama and Amber were putting the food onto the table for everyone to dig in. As much as I hated being at home, I missed my mama's cooking. No one cooked like her. I sat down next to Sean as he began preparing my plate. I looked into his face. I loved Sean or at least the Sean that I was hoping he would become. But at the same time, my heart was starting to beat for Antwan, a guy who made it perfectly obvious that he needed me in his life. But still, the heart wants what the heart wants. As confused as I was, I wasn't confused about the way I felt about Sean. I loved him, but I knew he wasn't ready for marriage. But if I didn't marry Sean, he would own rights to everything that Antwan worked his whole life to achieve. Antwan hated A.J. Miller. If marrying Sean helped Antwan, why not do it? What did I really have to lose?

"She made this bed, too, Hanna. She needs to lie in it." My mother told Ms. Lee over lunch that afternoon, after tensions settled a little.

"Well, I see no use in making up a bed that's going to end up messed up again anyway." Ms. Lee rolled her eyes over from my mother to her son.

"Amen on that." Amber agreed.

"They are just kids. She doesn't even know what she wants, and it's apparent that Sean doesn't either!" Ms. Lee exclaimed. "And if she accepts the proposal that you told the entire tristate area that she was accepting, when did you all plan on getting married?"

Sean looked at me. "July 4th."

I looked at him. That was the day his brother was killed. I looked at Ms. Lee who tried her best to remain emotionless.

"That's too soon." Ms. Lee looked at my father for his opinion.

"You've sat there, quiet this entire evening, only saying a few sentences to your young daughter, who is about to ruin her life marrying someone who is nowhere near being ready for this!"

My gaze met my father's.

He cleared his throat, his cognac brown eyes searching my face.

"This is their life, Hanna. You don't control it, I don't control it. The best thing we can do is stay out of it and let these two handle this."

Ms. Lee had this 'nigga, what' look on her face before she went in on his ass.

I sighed as my phone vibrated on my lap. I looked down at it. It was a message from Sean's sitting-right-next-to-me ass. I rolled my eyes before checking the message.

"Where were you last night?" it read.

THE LYRICS TO HIS SONG

I glanced up at Sean before looking down at my phone. It was heard as fuck lying to that nigga. Ugh. There was no way I could have told that nigga that I was with Antwan all night. There was no way that he could ask me what happened, and I could lie, telling him, oh, nothing, knowing good and got-damn well that Antwan's lips sucked the life out of me. That I still felt Antwan's silky lips stroking mine. Sean knew all of my secrets and all of my weaknesses… Except for this one. I think I'd just keep this one to myself.

"Working on music." I texted, which was the truth. "I dropped my phone in some water. Guess I'll have to use the new iPhone that Karen gave me, which I left in Karen's office by accident yesterday." Which was the truth as well.

I didn't think Sean believed me, but he got to the point. "Marry me, boo." he texted.

I looked up at Sean, whose eyes were tracing my lips. Then, I sighed, texting back.

"Sean, you need help. You need rehab, and you need therapy too." I pressed send.

Sean looked down at his phone as it lit up, our parents arguing, Amber laughing at the three of them talking about Sean and I as if we weren't sitting right there.

Sean shook his head, tapping his iPhone with his fingers.

The display on my phone read, "Nah, all I need is you."

I shook my head at him before texting and sending, "Sean, you don't even remember what you did to me. I can't even poop without pooping out blood, Sean! You choked my ass to sleep! And you don't even remember. And you don't think you need help?"

After reading the message that I sent, Sean's eyes widened a little before looking up at me. He shook his head in disbelief.

I nodded.

Sean texted me, "Audrey, bae, that wasn't me. You know that's not who I am. I'm sorry for hurting you that way. You did nothing to deserve that." He looked at me after sending the message.

I sighed after reading his text, texting my life away. "Call your doctor Monday, get a referral to a psychologist. Get some help. Accepting your ring—should I chose to accept it—is not my final decision, Sean. You getting better and putting forth the effort is. You already know that I love you. But love isn't always enough. You were so mad at me the other night. No Vaseline, Sean. You know you've got a big ass muthafuckin' dick, Sean! A part of me hates you, whoever you are."

Sean read my texts, taking a few deep breaths before responding back. "I don't wanna lose you."

"Then show me something different, Sean, or you will." I sent to him.

Sean looked at me, his temples twitching.

"The fuck y'all doing over there? Texting when you're sitting right next to each other?" Amber called us out.

"Well," I rolled my eyes at my sister, "if our parents weren't talking about us like we weren't sitting here, then maybe Sean could say what he has to say. Y'all wanted to get together and have lunch, so he could propose to me the proper way, whether I said yes or no. Yet, y'all are bashing the situation instead of giving your blessing, which is the impression you all gave him when you told the boy that you wanted him to propose to me in front of you all over lunch. Ms. Lee, if you're not giving your son your blessing, you could have saved yourself some gas money and stayed your ass in Richmond."

Amber laughed out loud.

Ms. Lee laughed a little too.

My parents seemed embarrassed.

"Well, it's about time you get some balls." Ms. Lee dug into her salad. "I wish you would have had some balls when Sean was staying out all night. Or maybe when he was cheating on you. Or maybe before he thought it was okay to sleep with your best friend, who was also your brother's girlfriend. Or maybe before he had two babies that you're just now finding out about. I'm taking up for your ass, and you have the nerve to talk shit to me?" Ms. Lee scoffed. "Your own mother could care less if you're happy or not, yet you have the nerve to pop off at the mouth?"

I shrunk back in my chair, not saying a got-damn thing in response because she was right. I came into that house with intentions on marrying Sean in hopes that maybe he would change for me. But after talking to the sister who never gave me a bit of sound advice in her life and finding out that marrying Sean would give me rights to Antwan's music, I had to step in to help. My parents were prime examples that marriage was only a business deal. That love didn't have shit to do with marriage. I wanted Sean to love me, but after Antwan kissed me the night before, I wasn't so sure it was Sean's love that I wanted.

Sean shook his head at his mother before turning to me. "This has nothing to do with them and everything to do with us. I messed up. I should've never messed around with Brenda or with Fatima or with anyone. I have always had a hard time showing you that I care about you, you know that. But you also know that I've always cared about you. That I've always loved you. We don't have to set a date yet; just give me some time to get myself together. Just say yes, that you want to marry me. That you'll never leave me. That you'll be mine forever. I know that I don't deserve your forgiveness, but I'm asking you for it. Please, Audrey."

182

THE LYRICS TO HIS SONG

I just looked at him, trying my best not to cry as he slid that velvet ring box out of his pocket. I wanted to believe every word that came out of his mouth, but I knew him. Once he had me where he wanted me, he was going to go back to being the same old Sean. The Sean who didn't love me until he ran out of options. I watched as Sean slid his ring onto my trembling finger. I flinched as my mother started taking pictures with her cell phone. I glanced at my father who was looking at me, waiting on my answer.

I looked at my mother, who just wanted to see her oldest daughter married to a man who would take care of her financially. Then, I looked at Ms. Lee who was as independent as they came, not needing a man for shit. Then, I looked at my sister who was tired of seeing me let others dictate my life. Then, I looked at Sean, whose facial expression said that he would change for me before he lost me.

I hesitated to nod, but nevertheless, it was a nod.

"Lord, Jesus." Ms. Lee shook her head as my mother clapped with joy.

"You will? You'll marry me?" Sean grinned, already pulling me closer to kiss him, something he hadn't done in a long time. I mean, he kissed me, but the kisses he gave weren't authentic. He always kissed me like he was kissing an old friend or some girl who he was just trying to hook up with for the night. But that day, the kiss he gave me was full of relief. Like he'd finally won something that he could be proud of.

The doorbell rang.

Amber looked at the two of us, shaking her head at the engagement. "I guess I'll get the door." She got up from the table. "It's probably the flowers that my boyfriend, Scott, said he was sending me today. We had plans tonight, ya know. If I leave in an hour, I can get back to Georgia just in time to still go out tonight." Amber strolled out of the dining room, on her way to answer the front door.

"So, what are you two kids getting into tonight?" Ms. Lee sighed, not sure what else to say after I went against her advice.

Sean shrugged. "Well, I really didn't have anything planned for shawty. We usually stay home and watch movies on her birthday/Valentine's Day. But," Sean squeezed my hand, "tonight, let's go on a cruise around the harbor. What do you think?"

I shrugged. I should have been happy to be engaged, but I didn't think I'd ever been more depressed. I looked down at the hand that he was holding, eying the huge diamond on my ring finger. It looked a lot better in the box than it did on my finger. It was heavy as hell. Not just on my hand but on my heart.

"Congratulations, honey!" Mama squealed, watching me eying my ring. "I need to call my mother!" Mama stood from the table just as Amber slowly entered the dining room, stopping in the doorway.

"Ummm…" Amber scratched between her pixie braids anxiously. "Sis, you have company." She stood in the doorway, her eyes as big as coasters. She looked back over her shoulder, standing aside as Antwan and Apollo walked through the doorway and into the dining room.

I gasped, eyeing the two brothers standing there, dressed in Givenchy urban attire. Antwan was dressed in all black, while his brother sported sky-blue; both had a purple bandana draped around their necks. I attempted to stand from the table, but Sean held my arm, grabbing me back to my seat. I looked at Sean as he let go of my arm and stood from the seat.

"Mama," Amber cleared her throat, "This is—"

Mama spoke up, "I know who they are," Mama snapped, looking Antwan in his face.

"What I don't know is why they're here, in my house, uninvited at that?"

Antwan grinned. "Good afternoon. I'm not trying to interrupt of intrude, but Karen Black says she's been calling shawty."

"Shawty'?" My mother scoffed.

"Miss Audrey all morning." Antwan continued. "We are performing tonight at my brother's club, and we need to practice, so…"

Our parents looked at me. Dad was furious. Ms. Lee looked like she was actually amused.

"Young man, we are having lunch." My father stood from the table, glaring at Antwan. "I don't give a got-damn who you are or how much money you make, you don't just storm into my got-damn house and think it's okay to disrespect my daughter in front of her fiancé. Get the fuck out of my house."

"Daddy!" I exclaimed, not believing my father, who almost never spoke up on anything, had the nerve to come off at Antwan that way. As if Antwan was the one in the wrong. Sean had done plenty of disrespectful shit to me throughout the years, that my father knew of, and never once had my father went off on him. I guess my father saw himself in Sean. And when he saw Antwan, I guess my father already knew Antwan's intentions were to steal me away from Sean. The same way that plenty of men had tried to steal Mama away from my father.

Antwan looked at me, glancing at my hand before I tried to slip it under the table. He shook his head and then looked back at my father. "I mean no disrespect to your house, sir. And I mean no disrespect when I say this either—fuck that ring." Antwan snarled. "That ring don't mean shit to me."

Sean tried to approach Antwan and his brother, but I jumped up from the table, pulling Sean back. "Sean, no, stop!" I yanked him back.

Sean looked back at me, looking at me like I needed to sit my ass back down in that got-damn chair and let him handle the situation before I got handled. "Audrey, you need to sit back down in that chair," Sean demanded.

I let go of Sean's arm, but I didn't sit down.

"We have a show to do tonight; that's the only reason I'm here. Ain't nobody intimidated by that lil' ring. I mean, it's cute, but she should have come to Jared." Antwan grinned.

Apollo smirked.

There I was, pulling Sean back again until he finally pushed me off of him and approached Antwan.

"I already told you that you don't want no problems, Antwan. I'ma ask you one more muthafuckin' time to leave my girl alone." Sean snarled in Antwan's face.

Antwan scoffed, 'nigga, you ain't shit' drawn all over his face.

"Oh, so you think because you bought her a ring that you own her; is that it? Why are you so threatened by me? If you're so sure that she belongs to you, then why are you so mad that I came to the party? It's because you know that I can walk out that door with 'your' girl. Oh, before I forget—" Antwan dug in his pocket, taking out the cell phone that I dropped in the pool at his apartment building. And he handed it to Sean.

Sean looked at it for a minute, glaring at it like he just knew that phone wasn't mine that Antwan took out of his pocket. "The fuck is this raggedy-ass shit?" Sean eyed the cracks that were all over the front of the screen. He knew it was mine; he just didn't want to believe it.

"Your girl left it at my crib yesterday after our little swim in the pool." Antwan could barely get the words out before Sean was reaching for the gun in his pants at the very same time that Apollo and Antwan were reaching for theirs.

Mama and Ms. Lee were screaming hysterically.

"Oh, hell nah! We ain't about to have that shit up in here! Sean, chill the hell out! Antwan, Apollo, y'all need to leave." Amber tried to defuse the situation, but it just kept getting worse.

Antwan looked into Sean's face. "It's obvious that shawty loves you. You don't deserve her, but that's your muthafuckin' ring on her finger. Regardless of what you think might have happened at my place last night, you're the one about to wife her. What I've got going on with your girl is strictly business, so watch ya self, homie. If I really wanted your girl, I'd already have her."

Sean's temples twitched, hand still over his gun.

Antwan looked over Sean's shoulder at me. "Lyric, you comin' or what?" Antwan looked back at Sean.

My family looked at me, shaking their heads at me with disapproval. All but Amber, who was behind me, pushing me forward. I looked at her over my shoulder.

"Girl, you better go," she whispered, shoving me in my back.

Sean turned around, facing me as I approached the three of them. Sean looked at me like I better not make another move, but I kept on walking until I was standing face-to-face with both Sean and Antwan, Apollo stepping to the side, chuckling to himself.

Antwan's eyes traced my silhouette in my sexy A-line dress before looking back at Sean. He grinned a little.

Sean turned to me. "Audrey, we have plans."

Amber shook her head at Apollo and Antwan. "No they don't."

Sean glared at my sister and then looked back at me, "You're really steppin' out with this nigga? This nigga is the reason why you didn't answer my calls last night? Audrey, are you—"

"Sean Justin Lee!" Ms. Lee called out to her son.

Sean looked back at her over his shoulder.

"Let the girl go. She's made it perfectly clear who she wants to be with, Sean. You're about to own the company that this so-called superstar works for," Ms. Lee boasted. "The employee has become the employer. I'm sure that must be hard for Antwan to deal with. Everything that he owns will become yours in a few days. I'm sure that must hurt."

Apollo and Antwan glared over at Ms. Lee, clicking their teeth.

Sean looked back at Antwan, grinning.

Antwan looked at him. "Yeah, I bet it hurts even more knowing that your wife will be working for me and not for him. That his wife is my employee. That I'll be the reason why she's working late hours. Yeah, best believe a nigga is gonna be working the shit out'cha wife. "

I pulled Sean back before those two, or should I say those three, starting firing at one another in my parent's dining room. "Sean!" I yelped, pushing Sean away from the twins, standing in between them.

Sean looked down at me, eyes glaring, temples twitching.

I looked at Antwan, who was looking down into my face, shaking his head at me like he couldn't believe I was giving my life to a man who wasn't ready for me.

Antwan looked at Sean, grinning before looking back at me.

"Aye shawty, are you done playing make-believe? Is you comin' or nah? We don't got all day."

THE LYRICS TO HIS SONG

CHAPTER SIX

Kill For Mine

There I was, jumping into the passenger seat of Antwan's white Chevy Tahoe that afternoon. The look on both my family's and Sean's face when I walked out that door with the twins though. What was I supposed to do? I already knew Antwan called himself trying to rescue me when he showed up to my parent's house. How he got my parent's address, I had no idea. But he came to get me, and that had to mean something. What it meant, I wasn't exactly sure. But something was telling me I was in for a strange chain of events.

"Damn, that's a big ass ring!" Apollo sat on the edge of the backseat, looking over my shoulder at my ring.

I rolled my eyes.

"Let me see that shit." Antwan grabbed my hand, looking at my ring before looking into my face, shaking his head once we got to a stoplight. "It's cute. It's got a few scratches underneath the surface though, kind of like your whack-ass relationship with this nigga." Antwan let go of my hand, taking off down the road as soon as the light turned green. His right hand gripped my thigh instead. That fool was trying his best to hike my skirt up a little higher so that he could feel my bare skin.

I gasped a little, grabbing his hand. "You both were out of line today. I can't believe y'all bogarted your way into my parent's house, crashing my engagement lunch. How the hell did you two even know where the fuck my parents lived in the first place?"

"Snare told us that Fatima was going over your parent's place for lunch today. I asked my nigga for the address, and he gave it to me. What did the bitch have to say about fuckin' around with ya nigga?" Antwan smirked.

I frowned at him. "Nothing that meant anything. Fuck her."

Antwan glanced at me. "You'll be a'ight, shawty. It won't always be this way. I promise. You should've told the nigga to keep that ring though. Why did you say yes? You know you wanted to tell the nigga to get the fuck on with that bullshit."

I looked at Antwan. "Speaking of bullshit," I changed the subject up real quick, "Brandie tells me she was blowing up your phone last night. What do you have her number saved as?"

Antwan made a face at me like he didn't have to tell me shit.

"Her number is saved under worry-about-ya-clown-ass-nigga-Sean-and-don't-worry-about-what-the-fuck-I-do."

I laughed in disbelief. "Oh, really? He's the clown, and you're the one who has my sister's number on speed-dial?"

Apollo sucked his teeth. "Man, fuck all that shit. Every muthafuckin' body has Brandie's number saved in their got-damn phone, but that don't mean a muthafucka answers that bitch. She's probably saved under Last Resort #1 or some shit. Antwan, shawty said yes; that's the end of that. On to the next. You know the routine, playboy. We've got business to attend to. I've got a track I want shawty to sing the hook for me with cuz tonight at my spot. We need to stop by my shawty's crib though to pick up my kids."

Antwan shook his head, looking at his brother. "You know I hate going over in that neck of the woods. Why the fuck do you stay out there in Meade Village, bruh, when you can be living it up with me? I've got plenty of cribs to choose from. Where you wanna stay? Baltimore? Essex? Towson? Georgetown? Alexandria? Hollywood? D.C.? Bethesda? Take your pick. You're stackin' all that bread, and you're still living like you're waiting on that welfare check to hit your mailbox."

"Nigga, I ain't forgetting where I came from. Ever." Apollo let his brother know.

"Chill. I'm not asking you to forget, bruh, I'm just asking you to move on. Don't you get tired of watching your back all the time? Shit, I do, nigga. Most of the trouble that I'm in has been from keeping you out of trouble! You know I'm gonna always look out for you, that's not even a question, but if you cared anything about a nigga, you'd leave this hood shit alone. You're a leader whose crew is reckless, dangerous, and has gotten far beyond your control! They stay robbin' niggas, they stay into it with Murk, and they stay killin' somebody. When you started this crew, y'all were just slangin', just hustling', just protecting your 'hood. Now? Shit, your crew is known for shootouts with entire neighborhoods, known for robbin' jewelry stores, known for raping women, and other shit. And your name is tied to that shit, nigga - whether you're involved or not!"

Apollo waved his brother off. "Man, my shit is on lock."

"Nah, your shit is all over the got-damn place. You got this phat-ass contract, where you don't even have to run the streets another day in your life, and here you go, chasing after this girl when she's not even worth being chased after. You've got two kids with this bitch, and every time you go over shawty's crib, there's always some shit with her. Shawty in the military, who stays on Fort Meade, is feeling the fuck out of you, and you're still sprung over McKaylah's stupid ass. I'm telling you, you ain't getting me in no shit today, Apollo!" Antwan told his brother.

And the shit started as soon as we stepped foot in McKaylah's apartment. I'd never seen a house so filthy. McKaylah was a shapely white girl with auburn hair and olive-toned skin. And she had a booty on her like she'd been eating cornbread all her life. There McKaylah was, looking like she was fresh off the cover of Elle magazine, and her house was looking like something off of Hoarders. I mean, there were pizza boxes, diapers, clothes, plates, forks, soda cans, toys, tissue, mail, some of everything on this girl's carpet. I was almost scared to step through her living room, afraid something was going to jump up and attack me.

Antwan shook his head at his brother and this girl as they argued, standing on top of a heap of trash.

"Nigga, I ain't seen you in weeks, and you think I'm just gonna let you roll up in my spot and take my kids?" McKaylah pushed Apollo in his chest. "My girl, Ashanti, told me she saw your trifling' ass at the club last night, bitches all in your face and shit, and you have the nerve to come up in here and talk shit about my place that I pay the bills for?"

"Man, ain't nobody tryin' to hear all that shit, McKaylah. I paid your muthafuckin' rent up for six muthafuckin' months. I bought some new furniture for this filthy muthafuckin' house a few months ago. I even paid some muthafuckas to clean this shit, and you got the house back lookin' like a muthafuckin' crack house, yo. The fuck you been doin' in here around my kids? Where my girls? Tia! Nika! Daddy's here!" Apollo called out.

"You're not taking my girls, Apollo!" McKaylah pushed him, her light skin turning red.

"Man, what do you care about my girls? My mans and them told me you had my kids knocking on the neighbor's door for food and shit! Man, what happened to the girl I used to know? The girl who cared more about her kids than how she looked? You're over here looking like a got-damn movie star, and your house looks like the inside of that got-damn dumpster outside! If my kids ain't lookin' like you, hair done, nails done, everything did, I swear, I'm beating all that makeup and weave off your muthafuckin' ass!" Apollo warned her.

And then, two of the most adorable little girls came running into the living room, racing through the junk. Apollo crotched down as they ran into his arms. They were laughing and crying all at once, happy to see him, like they hadn't seen him in ages. Apollo hugged his girls, looking them over as if he was checking for bruises or marks of any kind that weren't there the last time that he saw them.

Apollo smiled, looking his giggly girls eye to eye. "How have my main misses been?"

"Fine!" They giggled, playing in their father's dreads.

"Are you taking us with you, Daddy?" The older of the two girls asked, her big, brown, hopeful eyes searching her father's face.

Apollo looked her over, eying the holes in her clothes, the fact that her pants were high water as hell, and the fact that her hair was up in a knotty ponytail that hadn't been combed in what looked like a week or two. Apollo's temples twitched, "Yeah, Nika, Daddy's taking you with me."

"The hell you are!" McKaylah scoffed, folding her arms.

"Daddy?" Lil' Tia's laughter faded as she tugged on her daddy's dreads a little. "Uncle Wale gave me a whippin' last night."

Apollo looked at Antwan and then back at his kids. "Uncle Wale?"

Tia nodded. "We hadn't eaten anything since breakfast, and I snuck into the refrigerator last night to get some Cheetos. Uncle Wale whipped me with that." Tia pointed to the extension cord that the big screen T.V. and DVD player were plugged into.

Apollo stood up from the floor, looking at McKaylah like he wanted to beat her with the got-damn extension cord. "You let this nigga beat my daughter with that shit, yo?"

"She's not telling you the entire story, Apollo." McKaylah rolled her eyes, giving him attitude, but you could hear her voice shaking. She was scared. Shit, I was scared. I had heard about Apollo. He didn't play when it came to family. And to hear that some other nigga—a family member who it sounded as if he didn't like all too much, was whipping his kids had to sting.

"I don't give a fuck what the entire story is. Why the fuck is this nigga putting his muthafuckin' hands on my daughter?" Apollo growled.

"He wasn't whipping your daughter; he was whipping his daughter!" McKaylah yelled.

My heart pounded in my chest. "Oh shit…" I muttered.

Apollo was stunned for a few seconds, not knowing what to do at that moment but look down at the two little girls who looked just like him.

Nika and Tia looked up at Apollo, not realizing what was going on.

"Uncle Wale is here, Daddy," Tia told Apollo. "He spent the night last night."

Apollo looked at McKaylah, who was already backing up, scared out of her mind after the news she'd just given Apollo. "Oh for real? Where's this nigga at?"

Moments later, this tall brown-skinned dude came strolling down the hallway, out of what looked like McKaylah's bedroom. He looked like the brown-skinned version of Antwan. Maybe a few years older than Antwan.

Both Apollo and Antwan looked at McKaylah before looking back at the guy.

"The fuck you doin' here at my girl's crib, nigga?" Apollo was ready to flex, but his little girls were grabbing onto him.

Wale grinned. "Nah, nigga, what are you doin' at my girl's crib? And you ain't going no got-damn where with my daughter."

Apollo pulled his 9-millimeter from his jeans. The little girls he believed to both be his were holding onto him like they weren't the least bit fazed that their father was holding a gun and ready to use that muthafucka.

"Come on, Apollo. Let's roll. Let's do what you came to do. Get'cha girls and bounce, nigga. As far as we're concerned, they're both your kids. Fuck him; shit, fuck this bitch, too!" Antwan tried to warn his brother. "I told you I wasn't getting into no shit withcha ass today, bruh. Come on; let's bounce!"

"Get my girls out of here, Lyric. Will you do that for me?" Apollo looked at me.

I didn't even hesitate. I wasn't about to get in the middle of the shit that I knew was about to go down. I went over and grabbed the little girls by their hands and took them outside of the apartment, hurrying to get them in the car and strapped in. I should have known something was up when the two were traveling without bodyguards, something Antwan wasn't known to do. They didn't want the bodyguards being witness to anything. I wished they would have thought the same about me. For whatever reason, they trusted me. I wasn't ready for any of the secrets that they were about to force me to keep.

Tia and Nika cried beside me in the backseat of the Tahoe, holding onto each other, crying in each other's arms. Two beautiful little girls caught in the crossfire of a woman who was sleeping with two men who were related. I wasn't sure if Wale was the twins' uncle or if he was their brother. Perhaps, one of A.J. Miller's children.

The next thing I heard was gunshots. The three of us screamed. Moments later, Apollo and Antwan come racing out of the apartment building. My heart was doing a high speed chase in my chest as the twins made their way to the truck. I knew Apollo shot Wale, or McKaylah, or both. There was no telling. I saw the blood splattered on his sky blue shirt as he jumped in the driver's seat, and Antwan jumped in the passenger seat. In seconds, Apollo was balling off down the road.

Antwan shoved his brother. "Muthafucka, I told you that I wasn't getting into any shit with your muthafuckin' ass today! I told you to quit fuckin' with this bitch years ago! That this bitch was no got-damn good! You should have been left this bitch alone! You didn't have to put the bitch's lights completely out, nigga!"

"Look how she had my got-damn kids living! I did everything for that muthafucka, and she was fuckin' around with Wale? Him, of all muthafuckas? Damn right I made it so that bitch won't play me or any other muthafucka!" Apollo yelled back.

"Nigga, you crazy! You can't leave them in there like that! You gotta get rid of—"

Apollo cut his brother off. "Look, let me handle it. Let me get y'all out of here and do what I need to do. Just chill, nigga."

"Nah, nigga, your crazy muthafuckin' ass needs to chill! Fuck!" Antwan yelled out. "You stay in some shit! You already know Pop's niggas are gonna find out you were over this bitch's house! Her neighbors are nosy as a muthafucka!"

Little Tia already knew something wasn't right. "Where is Mommy?" Tia cried.

"In hell." Apollo told the little girl, who couldn't have been older than four. Apollo glanced back at me, watching my chest heave in and out. "Can you call you girl, Mariah, and see if I can drop you and the girls off at her crib? There's no telling who saw you coming out of McKaylah's crib. The first place they're gonna look is your crib, shawty. It'll take 'em a minute to look over your home girl's crib."

I remembered what Mariah said about having sex with her roommate all day. "She lives with a roommate. They have plans today, hun. It's Valentine's."

"Please." Apollo begged. "Shit is about to get hectic. I know it is. Please, just do this one thing for me. Keep my girls out of this shit."

Antwan looked back at me, his eyes apologizing for getting me involved.

I sighed as Antwan handed me all three electronics that I'd left on Karen's desk the day before. I called Mariah and then gave Antwan Mariah's address so he could call his bodyguards to tell them where to meet him. When we got to Mariah's condo, Mariah was standing outside in sweats, as if she'd just finished jogging. She took her ear buds out of her ear as she watched me get out of the truck with the little girls.

Antwan got out too. And we watched as Apollo sped out of the parking lot in his brother's car.

"The fuck is going on?" Mariah watched Apollo balling down the street. Mariah looked down at the girls and then at Antwan.

"Apollo found out his girl was fuckin' around with our brother." Antwan shook his head.

I knew it.

"So," she stared down at Apollo's kids. "What is this nigga about to do?"

"Shit, he's already done it, no hesitation, no questions." Antwan exhaled deeply. "Wale told him he wasn't going anywhere with his daughter. Apollo said which daughter. Wale said Tia. And you already know what happened next. I didn't even have a chance to react. Apollo has been there for these girls through everything. He straight flipped on them muthafuckas. He shot Wale and turned and shot." Antwan looked down at his nieces, who were crying their pretty eyes out. "My brother doesn't play. Shit is about to get real deep, real quick."

Mariah looked at me, running my hands through my curls anxiously. She saw my ring and instantly grabbed my hands. "Wow, that is some birthday present! I hope that's what this shit is! I know this isn't an engagement ring, Audrey!"

I rolled my eyes, slipping my hands from hers.

Antwan scoffed. "Man, whatever. I came by your parents' place to take you out for your birthday, shawty. I could give a fuck about that fake ass proposal. I wanted to swing by my place for a while, show you a little of Twan's World before we went to rehearse your hook for this song I wrote about you."

I just looked at Antwan, heart skipping.

"It's called Your Lips." Antwan grinned through his pain.

"Uh-oh. A song based on true life experiences, huh?" Mariah looked at my lack of ability to look into his face when he mentioned the name of the song.

"Queen wrote the hook for me this morning. I know you said you didn't wanna be in the spotlight, but I'm not trying to hire another background singer. You and my cousin are all I need. I gotta go catch up with my brother. I already know where he's headed, yo. I still gotta stay on schedule. Still gotta do my thang. I'm not getting caught up in my brother's shit this time around, shawty. We have some people coming to the club tonight. Might go into business with Chopper Lewis, you know, the CEO of Beat the Block Records. He's got some heavy hitters on his label. I'm thinking about joining forces with him. Meet me at my brother's club at around seven, so we can rehearse. The show starts at nine. I think we have enough time to rehearse. Tell your boy he can roll through, too."

Antwan reached for a hug from his nieces and received hugs and kisses from both. "Take care of my nieces, a'ight? I gotta call my aunts from Tallahassee. I'm sure they'll come up to get the girls until shit is settled. I'll catch y'all later."

We watched Antwan jump in his Navigator, and his bodyguards get him down the road, on his way to clean up whatever mess his brother made. I was nervous as hell and really couldn't handle anymore drama that day, but there I was, immersed in it. Mariah wasn't letting me go to the club alone, knowing shit was about to pop off. Apollo killed A.J. Miller's son. Though Apollo was A.J.'s son too, everyone knew they couldn't have been further than family. Blood meant nothing to the two of them.

Mariah's roommate/playmate, Breazy, agreed to watch the girls while we went out that night to Rhymes. I really was in no mood to rehearse for a show that I wasn't planning on being in. Why was shit happening so fast? Just two days earlier, I was stacking shoes at Foot Locker. All of a sudden, I was signing a contract with a superstar who everyone was dying to get to know. I was a songwriter, who could sing a note or two. Nothing special to me, but everyone around me wanted me to showcase my talents. I was a behind-the-scenes type of person who hated the spotlight. But Antwan wanted me right next to him. True, I recited poetry on stage every now and then, but I wasn't ready to travel the world. And I damn sure wasn't ready to be a witness to a murder. Antwan and Apollo were about to go about their business like nothing happened. Like Apollo didn't just kill his baby's mama and his own brother. I wasn't ready. I should have listened to Sean's jealousy that day.

I didn't invite Sean, but damn it if he wasn't there at the club, waiting on me. The place was packed, but there was no avoiding Sean. He was standing alongside the wall, in the hallway entrance to the club. He grabbed me as soon as I tried to get past him. He'd changed from the attire he wore to my parent's house, and he was back in his street attire. Rocking all that purple from head to toe. Sean held my hand in his, looking down at his ring like he was making sure I hadn't taken it off.

"She has to get to rehearsal, Sean," Mariah hissed, locking her arm around my arm, pulling me from Sean.

Sean looked her over and then clicked his teeth before looking at me. "I thought you already rehearsed earlier?"

I swallowed hard.

"She did, nigga, over at my crib with Queen." Mariah rolled her eyes.

"Was I talkin' to your ass, Mariah? I was talkin' to my fiancée." Sean snapped at Mariah.

"You need to get some business, shawty, so you can stay the fuck out of Audrey's. Damn. Get the fuck on, yo."

Mariah was about to pop off at the mouth as usual.

I cut her off before she caused a scene. "Boo, let me talk to Sean. I'll see you backstage."

Mariah shook her head. "Nah, bruh, I'm staying right here with you." She rolled her neck from me to Sean, looking him over before looking into his face, her lips pursed.

Sean shook his head at her before looking back at me. "Nah, yo. You went over Apollo's baby mama's crib, didn't you?"

I hesitated.

"The police are backstage questioning your nigga. They wanna question your ass too, Audrey." Sean shook his head. "You wanted in this life, so now you're in, shawty. I told you fuckin' with them niggas were bad news. Go handle your business, Miss Know-it-all. Let's see how much you know when you're behind bars with these niggas." Sean shook his head at me.

I looked into Sean's face, my heart pounding.

"McKaylah's sister found blood all over McKaylah's living room this afternoon." Sean tried to read my nervous facial expression.

I kept quiet. Apollo went back and got rid of the bodies that afternoon, but apparently he didn't clean the apartment good enough.

"Neighbors say they saw Antwan, Apollo, his little girls, and a brown-skinned girl with curly hair and a tight polka-dot dress get into a white Chevy Tahoe." Sean looked at me. "Were you with them niggas in Meade Village apartments this afternoon? Because if you were, they're gonna put your dumb ass in this bullshit, Audrey!"

I didn't know what to say except, "Sean, I don't know what you're talking about."

"A'ight, when the police question you, you make sure you tell them muthafuckas the same thing." Sean shook his head at me.

"Nigga, bye." Mariah smacked her lips, pulling me away by my arm. "Keep calm, boo, and let's go see what this muthafucka is talking about."

"Man, Detective Ramos, I don't know what the fuck you're talking about." We heard Antwan's voice as we entered backstage that night. Antwan, Drizzle, Rhandy, Queen, and the rest of Antwan's band were backstage that night, being questioned by a few detectives. They glanced at us as we entered the room.

"McKaylah Carmichael and Wale Miller are both missing! Their blood is all over that apartment! Witnesses say that they saw you go into that house with your brother." The detective glanced at me and then looked back at Antwan. "We have witnesses who know the exact outfit that you both had on, so don't even try to lie, Antwan."

Antwan clicked his teeth. "Yeah, I took my brother over shawty's crib to get his kids."

"What time was that?" another female detective asked.

"Around 1:30 this afternoon, Detective Creech." Antwan exhaled deeply.

"And then where did you go?" Detective Creech looked at me and Mariah as we strolled into the room, standing alongside the wall.

"He was with me." I spoke up. "We went by my girl's place to write a few songs." I held up my lyrical journal.

Antwan looked at me, shaking his head. He didn't want me involving myself, but I was already involved. I hated to leave Antwan when he needed me. Getting caught up in his brother's drama was the last thing Antwan needed. His career was taking off; he was about to start a company, and he was going on yet another tour after already being on the road non-stop for damn near seven months. He didn't know I accepted Sean's proposal just so I could help him. Before that kiss Antwan gave me, I actually thought I could save Sean by marrying him. But after Antwan's lips touched mine, I wasn't so sure it was Sean who needed saving.

"Mr. Jared, we will be back. Your brother has gotten you into enough trouble. Don't take the wrap for this one." Detective Ramos sighed before leaving backstage with the other detectives.

I walked up to Antwan, watching him watch the detectives leave.

Antwan looked down into my face. "Why did you tell them muthafuckas that you were with me?"

I shrugged. "Sean says some people already saw me today."

"Yeah, but they didn't know your name, shawty. Your name wasn't put in this shit. I'm the one caught up in my brother's shit, Lyric. You should've just stayed out of it." Antwan leaned back against the wall that he was standing in front of.

I shook my head. "Nah, Antwan, you're not alone."

THE LYRICS TO HIS SONG

Antwan looked down at the ring on my finger and then back into my face, shaking his head at me. "Whateva, Mrs. Lee. A'ight, y'all. Time to rehearse." He turned from me, facing his crew.

I couldn't lie. I was really feeling the hook to the song, but I wasn't feeling singing the verse that Antwan was trying to make me sing in front of Sean. It pretty much gave away what happened the night before. Antwan wasn't playing any games. His agent showed up backstage that night, along with his publicist who was Beat The Block Records' publicist as well. They were loving my look, said it was the look that the company needed. That if Antwan wanted to appeal to a broader audience, he had to soften up his look a little. They told him that they watched my performance on YouTube and were looking forward to working with me but that I had to lose the nervousness and step my game up if I expected to perform with someone as big as Antwan Jared. They thought I was good but needed a vocal coach and a lot of work on my stage presence. That I needed to loosen up and relax. How the fuck could I loosen up and relax when I had so much going on? Too much going on, too fast.

"Your hips, your thighs, your lips got me feeling like this. Ooohh, I can't get enough; you got me feeling you when our lips touch." Queen sung the lyrics to the hook, along with the band.

I bobbed my head, standing up against the wall, reading over the lyrics. It was about 8:30. Elle swung backstage, bringing me a change of clothes. She brought me a pair of tight black pants and a lace fitted shirt to wear, with a pair of patent leather Red Bottoms. I hated wearing heels, but since I was going to be sitting on a stool, in the background with Queen, then it was all good. My heart beat out of control as Elle brushed my hair up into a ponytail, and Mariah redid my makeup.

"Girl, this tour is about to be off the chain!" Mariah spoke softly as the band practiced. "We go on tour in a week, girl. Shit, next Saturday to be exact." She shook her head. "Apollo's album drops next week too. He's going on tour with us. So much for rehab, you already know Sean is going on tour with them. The nigga is always making promises to you that he can't keep."

I sighed.

"And aren't y'all supposed to be in the studio putting together Antwan's new album? They're working the shit out'cha ass. Shit, other than the paycheck, it feels like we never left Foot Locker!" Mariah rolled her eyes, thinking of all the shit we put up with back at Foot Locker.

I watched as Antwan rapped his verse, facing his band, bopping his head, and swaying to his music. I always loved to see Antwan perform, whether it was live or on television. He put everything he had into his raps. The lyrics weren't always my favorite, but his delivery was on point. This song wasn't so bad, since it was about me. My nerves were on edge once it was time to take the stage. My girls wished me luck as we passed them and went on stage. I sat alongside Queen on a stool a few feet behind Antwan. Queen grinned at me, her bright red lips juicy as hell. She winked her eye at me before looking out at the crowd of people.

The place was lit like a muthafucka. Antwan performed at his brother's club every weekend that he was in town to help his brother generate more business. Apollo was new on the rap scene and needed his brother's fan base to help boost his. Apollo was known in the streets, but Antwan was known worldwide. You would have thought there would have been jealousy or at least envy between the two, but their relationship couldn't have been further from hate. They fed off each other's energy. I saw evidence of that when I walked in on them in the studio that day. Nevertheless, Apollo kept Antwan in trouble, which made me question whether or not the fame was really what Apollo wanted.

"Look at ya nigga." Queen nudged my shoulder, whispering in my ear.

I looked in the direction that she nodded her head in, seeing Sean sitting at a booth to the right of the stage, my sister and a few other dancers sitting in the booth with him. I sighed as Antwan looked back over his shoulder at me. The crowd was hype, waiting for Antwan to open his mouth and spit something a cappella, as he often did before the beat dropped.

"Aye, yo, you already know my twin, Antwan, is about to spit fire, so just sit back, relax, get high, and enjoy the ride!" Apollo hyped the crowd up even more, announcing his brother's presence over the microphone.

Apollo stood at the bar with a group of his boys from The Village. Despite the events that occurred that day, neither brother looked fazed. I, on the other hand, was anxious as hell. I just knew something crazy was going to happen. I sensed it the moment that I saw the police questioning Antwan backstage. I eyed Apollo, who wasn't dressed in purple that afternoon, but light blue from head to toe. I wasn't into that thug life, but I'd been around Sean and his homies enough to know that the street crews always changed their crew colors the day they knew some shit was about to pop off. That was in case the police showed up to wherever the chaos broke out; the street crews wanted to confuse the police, so they wouldn't immediately know which street crew was responsible for the street war.

I watched Antwan turn his white baseball cap, which looked neon blue under the white lights of the club, to the side. He placed his mic to his lips. "Now, tell me what nigga don't want a girl he can call his own? A girl whose touch will make you feel at home. Just when you thought no one understood what you need, this girl enters your life, has your heart racing at full stampede. In a perfect world, she'd already be mine. But I'ma get my shit together; yeah, perfection takes some time..."

Antwan looked over his shoulder and winked at me as the crowd whistled and squealed.

I swallowed hard as Queen nudged me. I looked over my shoulder at Elle and Mariah, who stood backstage, giving me a thumbs up like some damn fools. Then, I looked to the right of the stage where Sean was sitting, looking pissed as a muthafucka, shaking his head at me as the beat dropped.

"Yo," Antwan laughed, "fuck this ballad shit. Let's get down to muthafuckin' business. Let me tell you what happened to your boy last night. Shawty had a nigga feeling so good, high as a muthafuckin' kite. We started kissing and touching; this girl is such a flirt. She told me to be gentle, then she pulled up her skirt. She spread the legs for me, said it's yours if you want it. Told me she ain't been drilled in a minute, so when you dive in, nigga, don't kill it. Told me to take the pussy, so I slid my dick up in it. Shawty gobbled the dick, rode the skin off the dick. That shit was so good, something a nigga will never forget. Oh, before I left her, I said, 'shawty, you got a man?' She said, 'Don't you see his picture on my nightstand?' I laughed when I looked at the picture; said, 'Oh you're Sean's girl? I knew you looked familiar.'"

My eyes widened.

The band laughed, still playing along with the lyrics that were so not the lyrics that we rehearsed just a few hours earlier backstage. Antwan had the whole crowd going crazy, wondering if this dude was rapping lyrics that were true. A few days earlier, no one knew that I was Sean's girl, but he made the announcement loud and clear over the airways the day before that I, Audrey Shanay Gibson, was his fiancée. And right in front of a crowd of at least five hundred people, Antwan let it be known that, even though his song may have over exaggerated our encounter the night before, there was a flirtatious encounter. And you already know, as soon as the dude started rapping, people already had their cell phones held high, recording the show.

"Oh, boy," Queen muttered to herself before she stood from the stool, sliding it to the side with her Monolo's. She took over the song, singing the hook to Your Lips, the song that we were supposed to be performing.

I sighed, standing alongside her, pushing my stool to the side as well, singing along with her. Antwan's ass was bold as a muthafucka. He was already in enough shit and really didn't give a fuck if he was about to be in some more. Sean may have not showed me much attention when he thought no one else was interested, but when anyone else showed interest in getting to know me, it was straight war with him. But for whatever reason, Sean remained calm that night. He slouched back in his chair, chrome fronts gleaming, not the least bit fazed by Antwan's insinuations. And that shit made me really nervous. Sean, calm? Never.

In seconds, right in the middle of Antwan's first verse, a group of unfamiliar faces strolled into the club, dressed in all black attire, red and black plaid bandanas covering their mouths. Murk was in the building. The signature bandanas gave them away. They came from all directions of the club, scattering like ants, moving quickly across the club floor, removing their bandanas after their presence was made known.

"Aye, yo, Apollo!" This dark skinned tall guy shouted as he pulled his bandana from his face.

Everything happened so fast. Before Apollo's crew could react, bullets started spraying everywhere. The crowd scattered, trampling over one another to get out of the club. I caught a glimpse of Sean getting my sister and her girls out of harm's way before firing back. Queen tried her best to pull me along with her, so we could escape backstage with the rest of the band, but my feet were planted on the ground. I watched as Antwan and his band members fired back at the niggas who were shooting up the place. Drizzle's crazy ass had an AK-47, firing on those muthafuckas. The crew always kept weapons on stage, tucked behind their equipment.

"Audrey!" Mariah screamed at me from backstage.

I watched as Apollo fired shots back at the crew, who apparently had come to take him out. And I watched as Apollo was shot, right between the eyes. As soon as Apollo was shot, Antwan was shot in his side. Regardless, Antwan kept on firing until his gun was empty. He pulled out the gun that was tucked in the back of his pants, firing back, backing up, making his way to me, grabbing ahold of me, getting me backstage and out of harm's way.

"What the fuck, shawty?" Antwan screamed, his chest heaving in and out.

My eyes widened as I looked at the blood gushing out of the wound in his side. "Antwan, you've been shot!"

"Get out of here! Go!" Antwan pushed me, trying to get me to leave out the back door with the rest of the crew.

"No!" I screamed. "You have to get to the hospital!"

"Nah!" Antwan's eyes were getting heavy, but he refused to give into the pain and fatigue of losing all that blood. "I'm not leaving my brother!"

"Homie, he's already gone." Antwan's friend, Trap, hated to tell Antwan, but someone had to.

Antwan yelled out as Trap and Drizzle grabbed their friend, trying to get him to leave out the back door with the rest of us. I think it took about five people to get Antwan out that door; he was fighting with everything he had to stay.

I sat in the backseat of Trap's Cadillac, listening to everyone going off, frustrated, mad that they weren't prepared for what happened that night. They should have known better. Apollo should have been prepared; he knew that killing A.J.'s son was going to lead to war as soon as word got out that Apollo had left McKaylah's place that night. If the police didn't get Apollo, A.J. Miller was going to find a way to get him.

Queen removed the scarf from around her head and handed it to me. Blood gushed through the spaces in my fingers as I applied pressure to Antwan's side.

"I'ma get them muthafuckas!" Antwan screamed as I pressed down on his side.

My heart stampeded in my chest as Trap raced down the highway on the way to the hospital. I hadn't even known that boy a week. How the hell did I get caught up in Antwan's life?

We got Antwan to the hospital. Mariah went back to her crib to get Apollo's girls to safety. She told me she was going to take the girls with her to Alexandria where her cousin, Tracie, lived. She would text me when she got there safety. Sean's ass texted me, trying to make sure that I was okay. I rolled my eyes and ignored his text. By the time we'd gotten to the emergency room, Antwan was in and out of consciousness. The young hospital staff was so busy ogling over Antwan in the emergency room that they couldn't even concentrate on the fact that the boy had been shot in his side.

Antwan stayed conscious long enough to get registered that night but passed out just before giving registration his birth date. We all watched as Antwan was rushed to surgery. He was bleeding pretty badly. Apparently, he was shot more than once in his side. We were all worried that the bullets might have hit a major artery or organ, but both went straight through. As soon as he was stitched up, we were able to see him. But he wasn't too ready to see us. As soon as he came to, he was throwing shit across the room. He was hurt, he was angry, he was pissed. He had to be sedated before we could go into his room.

The staff was still pretty thirsty once Antwan was bandaged and sedated, hooked up to a bag of O-negative blood and fluids to keep him hydrated. Antwan lay in the hospital bed, temples twitching, but calm.

"Look, bitch. Are you gonna take his blood pressure? Or you gonna drool all over the muthafucka?" Queen hissed at the technician in triage that night.

The little thirsty bitch wiped the drool from her pink lips as she began taking Antwan's blood pressure. "I'm so sorry. I'm just—I'm just a huge fan." The technician looked Antwan's biceps over. She shook her head to herself at how fine that boy was.

I sighed. "Do you think he'll be able to go back home tonight?" I asked, eying the expression on Antwan's face. On second thought, nah, he didn't need to go anywhere. He was sedated, but that boy was heated. He was going to act a got-damn fool as soon as he left that hospital.

"I think the doctors are going to keep him here for a while, at least until tomorrow. I think he had a bad reaction to the medication that was given to him while they were stitching him up." The technician looked Antwan's face over before taking out a thermometer to take his temperature. "Mr. Jared, can you open your mouth please?"

Antwan looked up at her, eyebrows lowering, connecting, forehead wrinkling. Antwan really didn't feel like being bothered. And I was sure a room full of people, friends or not, was irritating his soul.

The technician sighed. "Well, we're about to move him up to room 336 in about ten minute. We'll check his vitals then."

Another technician entered the triage. "I think we need to move him like now. The lobby is filled with hundreds of people that found out that he was here! His bodyguards are standing by in the hallway, and hospital security is in the lobby, but you know how it got the last time that he was here!"

"Right." The drooler agreed with her co-worker. "Call a transporter down."

"Bodyguards?" Antwan's voice was weak. "Where were those muthafuckas when my brother got shot the fuck up?"

Drizzle and Trap looked at their friend.

"Antwan, about three of your bodyguards died trying to protect both you and your brother." Drizzle hesitated to say. "They died doing their muthafuckin' job; believe that, homie."

Antwan looked at him, his eyes watering. "Body—" Antwan choked, unable to get the word out. "Who did they get?"

"Gavino, Roland, and Oscar." Drizzle watched as Antwan went at it again, trying to snatch his IVs out. And there his friends were again, trying to calm him down.

Queen paced the floor that night in the lobby on the third floor.

"Well," Sheena Turner, Antwan's agent, stood in the doorway of the lobby, shaking her head, her brown skin glistening, "I'm glad Antwan is okay. I'm not trying to be greedy, but he has a lot of business ventures going on. This doesn't look good for him. What company wants to invest in a man whose life is so chaotic? Trying to hook up another meeting with these people is going to be very difficult."

Queen rolled her eyes. "This is the main reason why I never wanted to get involved with this industry bullshit. Y'all are always worrying about your own personal gain than worrying about a man who just lost his twin brother! I grew up with these two; they are the only brothers that I know! And you're over here worried about my nigga getting involved in more contracts with more greedy muthafuckas! Please, get the fuck on, Sheena. I've had enough of you for one day. You already know that I can't stand you! What happened back at that club is no different than what happens in this industry every day! You knew my brother was about to be owned by A.J. Miller, and you didn't even tell him." Queen shook her head at Sheena.

Sheena shook her head, grabbing her jacket and purse from the chair alongside the door. "When Antwan wakes up, tell him that I will be praying for him and his brother. I'll call him in a few days. Tell him to stay out of trouble."

Everyone shook their heads, knowing good and well Antwan's ass didn't know what staying out of trouble meant.

"Man, this shit isn't gonna die down this easy." Rhandy sat down in a seat across from me, popping open a bottle of Mountain Dew. "You already know 'Twan is gonna roll out as soon as he gets the fuck up out this bitch... and I'm rollin' with my nigga, too. Real talk, yo."

"Nigga, you must've lost your mind. Apollo dumped McKaylah's and Wale's body in the dumpster outside of Relentless Records. The janitor caught Apollo ballin' off out of the parking lot. Y'all already know A.J. sent these niggas after Apollo. And this nigga is about to take over Instinctive. He's about to make Antwan's life hell!" Snare warned his friends before they decided to get froggy. "Nigga, you wanna get froggy with this muthafucka? Go ahead and jump out there like a dumb ass if you want to."

"You already know 'Twan isn't gonna let this shit go, yo. I'm not about to let him face this shit alone! Hell nah! After all he's done for us? Hell nah, nigga." Drizzle was down to ride too. "Even little Lyric over here is down to ride with this nigga. You see she didn't leave him. I'm sure Antwan noticed her dedication too. He's pissed right now, but he sees you, shawty."

Everyone looked at me, nodding in agreement.

I exhaled deeply, looking down at my new iPhone as it vibrated. I'd received the, "We made it to cuzzo's place. The girls are safe, fed, and took a bath, boo. Oh, and I've got Steel's badass with me. If he pees on my couch, you bought it, bruh" text from Mariah. I was a little relieved.

"Hush! LOL Thanks, love. I'll call you soon. Antwan is resting." I texted back with a smooch emoji.

The doctor entered the lobby.

We all stood from the chair.

"Antwan is fine. He's responding very well to the blood that we're giving him. He asked me to tell you all to go home. He doesn't feel like company right now." Doctor Tabu knew we all hated to hear that he wanted us to leave.

We all looked at one another before gathering our things so that we could leave.

"Oh, I'm sorry, he wanted you to stay." Doctor Tabu cleared his throat.

Everyone looked at me.

I swallowed hard. "Me?"

Dr. Tabu nodded. "Yes, he said he wanted the one with the black lace top to stay with him. That he needed you here. He said something about wanting to hear your heartbeat. Probably metaphorically speaking, but he was adamant about you, and only you, staying."

CHAPTER SEVEN

Love on the Bench

I knocked on Antwan's room door before entering his room. Antwan was sound asleep, laying on top of his sheets, dressed in a clean tank top and boxers, probably some shit one of the thirsty nurses bought him because none of us left his side that night until he asked everyone to leave. I eyed the clothes sitting in a bag on top of the sink countertop in his room. They washed the dude's clothes, had the whole room smelling like Downy.

I shook my head, closing the door behind me, careful not to wake him. I went over to Antwan, taking the white throw blanket from the foot of the bed, pulling it over him. I looked over his handsome face before kissing him on the forehead. Then, I kicked my heels off and sat in the chair alongside his bed. I must've dozed off because, when I opened my eyes after what felt like seconds, Antwan was sitting up in his bed, looking at what I thought was his cell phone.

I sat up in my chair, rubbing my eyes.

Antwan looked at me before looking back down at the phone.

"Your nigga has been texting you for an hour."

I looked down at the pocket of my jacket that hung over the arm of the chair, which was the last place that I saw my phone. Then, I looked back at Antwan. "Is that my phone?"

"Yeah," Antwan looked at me before tossing my phone back to me. "I texted him back, told him that you were with me. That I fucked you to sleep."

My eyes widened as I looked down at my phone, immediately powering on the screen to see what the fool had written back to Sean. When I searched my messages for the past hour, they were all from Mariah. I looked up at Antwan, who grinned a little, before he stood from the bed. Even through his pain, he still had jokes.

"That's really not funny, Antwan." I shook my head at him.

"Yeah, it is. Fuck that lame ass nigga. Texting you instead of coming to check up on you, to make sure you didn't catch a bullet. I told you that ring don't mean shit." Antwan scoffed.

I watched his face grimace as he stood from the bed, hooked to his IVs. I rushed to his side, though he was waving me off like he didn't need any help. I bent over, unplugging the unit the IVs were hooked up to. "Antwan, you need help; you're hurt."

"I'm not dead, shit. I gotta pee. What'cha gonna do, shawty—hold my dick for me? Shit." Antwan scoffed.

I sighed, watching him slowly make his way towards the bathroom. Dude didn't even close the door; he could care less if I watched him using the bathroom. I sighed, turning my head, sitting on the edge of the hospital bed, listening to him drain himself. Even the sound of his pee was music to my ears. I guess I was just so happy to see that he was physically okay. I knew he was hurting inside. I knew he wanted to see me because he felt like I was a part of him. He'd known the others that he'd turned away all of his life. He'd only known me for a few days. But I'd admit, it did feel a whole lot longer.

I heard the water to the sink running, so I knew that he was finished relieving himself. I looked up at him as I watched him drying his hands before turning towards me, leaving the bathroom.

"Your friends are worried about you, boo." I told him.

"So is your friend. Shawty was texting to see if you were okay, Lyric." Antwan made his way over to the bed, sitting down next to me.

I bent over, plugging his IV unit back in.

"I texted her back, told her that you were asleep." Antwan looked my face over a little, his eyes watering.

"Why did you send your friends away, Antwan? They would have stayed here all night, no food, no sleep, nothing, to make sure that you're straight. And you told them to leave? Why?" I asked.

"Yo, I just ain't trying to deal with them. I have enough thoughts in my head and they keep trying to fill my head with more." Antwan's temples twitched. "My niggas have been texting me all night."

I looked at him. "All night? How long have I been asleep?"

"About three hours." Antwan watched my eyes widen. "Those got-damn nurses have been in here about thirty times since you've been asleep. One of them even offered to give a nigga a sponge bath." Antwan shook his head. "I told the bitch to get the fuck on. My brutha and the bodyguards that died protecting a nigga just got blown the fuck away, and these bitches still trying to get dicked down. My nieces have to grow up without a daddy, and these bitches in here thinking about fuckin'. Fuck!"

I shook my head, trying not to laugh at the thirst, not the situation.

"Antwan, you know the thirst is real. They just wanna make Antwan Jared feel better."

"Man, whatever." Antwan shook his head to himself. "I don't think I'll ever be myself again. I'm trying not to go straight berserk on these niggas but... those were my niggas. I have known Gavino and them all my life. That's my brother who took a bullet to the head. He left me, and that muthafucka knew he was all I had left of her! He knew I needed him! And he left me! He knew what was going to happen when he—" Antwan choked back the tears. "I'ma get them muthafuckas, Lyric. When they don't expect it, that's when I'ma get 'em. I'ma lay low for a little while, but I put this on everything, I'ma get them muthafuckas."

I shook my head. "That's not gonna bring him back."

Antwan looked at me.

"Antwan, honey, he was wrong, and you know it. He should've just took his daughters and left. It didn't have to happen that way, boo, and you know it." I had to tell him. "I know you miss him; I know you love him, but he's gone, Antwan, and going on a killing spree isn't going to change that."

"Do you know why Apollo killed his girl? It wasn't only because he was angry, but it was because McKaylah told Apollo that Wale raped her a few years ago. And to find out she was fuckin' around with that nigga after she accused him of raping her was what sent him over the edge. Little Tia was his heart. And to find out that she wasn't his, man, that damn near killed him. I told him back when Tia was born to take those girls from that bitch. That she was going to be the death of him. But he just couldn't move on." Antwan wiped the tears that started to slide down his face. "Women have always been our downfall. That's why I'm like fuck love and anything to do with it." Antwan looked down at the ring that I was wearing and then back into my face. "Love is not going to be the death of me, Lyric. Do you fuckin' hear me? If that's what you're looking for, you're not gonna find it in me, and you're damn sure not gonna find that shit in Sean. Fuck that nigga. If he's who you want, then go be with him."

My eyes glistening, watching the tears fall from Antwan's eyes. And I held his face in my hands, drying his tears. Antwan took my hands from his face and then laid down in the bed, turning from me. I laid down beside him, his back facing me. And I slid my arm around his waist, laying as close to him as I could so that he could feel my heart beating, his mother's heart beating. Antwan turned to me, grabbing me close, face pressed against my neck as he pressed his chest against mine. My heart beat just as hard as his heart did.

"Why, Audrey?" Antwan whispered before crying out loud.

"Man, he's gone! My brother's gone! Why? God, why? Why did you take them from me! Please, give them back to me!"

I cried with him, rubbing my hands across his smooth close-cut hair. "Oh, sweetie, I'm so sorry.

***

Antwan paid for the funeral costs for his brother and his three bodyguards, and Apollo's manager and producer, Trey Benson, paid for Apollo's wake. Antwan refused to go to it. It was more like a concert than a wake to me. The place was packed beyond capacity. Recording artists from BAM, Inc., were performing. The only person there who gave a heartfelt speech was Queen. She made it halfway through her speech before breaking down and crying. Drizzle, Snare, Rhandy, and Trap were too shook up to say anything. Apollo's entire squad was at the wake, dressed in purple to bid their leader farewell. Sean showed up, wearing Apollo's signature plaid white and purple shirt. It was almost as if he was letting everyone know that he was taking Apollo's place as their leader. There he was, about to go work for the man who was responsible for Apollo's death, yet there he was, rockin' Royal's colors and taking a spot that he'd wanted to be in ever since we were kids. I wasn't sure whose side Sean was on, but I would soon find out.

The funeral was held Friday, around eleven in the morning. It was not a service that I was looking forward to, as if any funeral was. I hadn't stepped foot into a church since my brother's memorial service, which was held just a few weeks after I woke up from my three-month-long coma. I was a little relieved that I missed my brother's closed-casket funeral; his face was mutilated from the car crash. Reporters were lined up in and out of the church, trying to get snap shots and interviews with both myself and my family members. They wanted to talk to the girl who had just woken up from a coma only to find out her brother was dead and she was saved by the heart of the Mayor of Baltimore City. Though it wasn't a funeral service, it was still pretty heart-wrenching. My father was sleeping with the pastor's wife at the church where my brother's service was held. There I was again, facing another bitch that my father was cheating with. I swore I'd never step foot in a church again unless it was for someone who couldn't make it without my support.

"Look at this hoe." Mariah nudged me in church that Friday as we watched Fatima strolling into church, hand and hand, with Snare.

I rolled my eyes at the bitch as she walked by, not even looking my way, though I knew she saw me sitting there in the fifth row of the church.

Sean didn't show up to the service. That was to be expected. He had business to attend to with A.J. Miller, who was also absent from the service. He went to Wale's funeral the day before, but somehow managed to miss Apollo's. The muthafucka couldn't even see his own son being put into the ground. Antwan's aunts in Florida refused to come and get Apollo's daughters. The girls took turns staying with me and with Mariah that week. Turned out, the family that his mother was visiting in Florida was A.J. Miller's family members. Turned out, Apollo and Antwan were raised by A.J. Miller's family. A.J.'s mother raised the boys until she died, leaving them to be raised by his brother, Queen's father. Antwan assumed that his mother's family raised him.

Judge Troy Michael showed up to the hospital that Monday that Antwan was released. He told Antwan that Apollo almost died the day that they were born. That there were so many drugs in his mother's system. His mother was trying to kill herself and her babies for whatever A.J. Miller and his family were putting her through. The judge couldn't even get around to telling Antwan how A.J.'s family ended up with Denise's children. He didn't want to hear anymore once he found out that his mother left him and his brothers with that evil family.

The worst part of the funeral service was watching Antwan break down over his brother's body as they lowered Apollo's body into the ground. Antwan dropped to his knees, crying out, cursing at the top of his lungs at God. My heart raced in my chest, and I rushed to his side, dropping to my knees right next to him. I surrounded Antwan in my arms, his tears soaking my shoulder.

Bright and early the next morning, I received a text from Karen saying that there was going to be a meeting at 8:30 that morning and that everyone needed to be there and on time. I was exhausted. Throughout that week, I was helping Sean move into his new place. The place that we were to move in once we were married. Between making sure Antwan was okay and helping Sean decorate his place, I was pooped. Not to mention, Sean started going to therapy that week as promised. Despite the fact that we were about to go on tour, Sean was scheduled to start rehab the first week of March. I wasn't sure if Sean's efforts to change were genuine or not. It seemed a little rehearsed. Seemed as though he was trying to compete for me, as if it were some game. I was in no mood for any meetings. I knew that a tour was coming up that Karen wanted me to take part in, even though I wasn't a part of any of the performances. She'd hired a background singer that week, since I was procrastinating on signing a singing contract with her. Tiara Knowles was her new background singer. Karen introduced me to her the day of Apollo's funeral. I guess Karen wanted me to meet my competition.

THE LYRICS TO HIS SONG

I got up, threw on a Marilyn Monroe fitted tee and denim tights and headed out the door. I stepped foot in Instinctive that day at the exact same moment that Antwan pulled up to the building. He was just as unenthusiastic to be at the building as I was. He looked like he'd been up all night, drinking and getting high. His eyes were low as hell, and he smelled like he tossed back a few pints of Hennessey. We didn't say anything to one another as we strolled down the hallway to Karen's conference room, Antwan's three new bodyguards following behind us.

We both stopped in our tracks after entering the double wooden doors of Karen's grand conference room. There, at the head of her table, sat A.J. Miller. And sitting to his left was Sean. I looked at Antwan who removed his blue baseball cap from his head.

"Come in." Karen looked at her watch. "It's 8:35. You're both late."

I glanced at Sean, who glared at Antwan, actually thinking we rolled in the spot together. I rolled my eyes before walking into the room, going over to stand alongside the wall with Mariah, who saved me a space beside her in the crowded room.

Antwan entered the room but didn't go any further than the wall alongside the entrance. He leaned back against the wall, hands in his pockets, like he had better things to do. "Can we hurry up with this bullshit ass meeting? I have better things to do with my time than be in the same room with the muthafucka who's responsible for his own got-damn son's death."

Karen sighed. "Antwan, now, what happened to your brother was tragic, but we can't go jumping to conclusions. You already know that Apollo was into it with Murk for years. And you already know that McKaylah's brother was their leader." Karen cut Antwan off before he could continue. "Apollo was A.J.'s son, just as you are, Antwan, so stop making this something that it's not. Can we get on with business and leave this family feud shit outside the door?"

Antwan's temples twitched as he leaned against the wall, waiting for her to go on with her speech. He glanced at A.J., who was sitting at the head of the table, a smirk swiping across his face. I swear, he looked like the chocolate version of Antwan.

"We are happy to announce our merge. It's happened a lot faster than anticipated. Our lawyers sat down and drew up new contracts for our companies. In six months, we will no longer be Instinctive Entertainment. We will take on Relentless as our company name. We will then draw up a new contract. I would like you all to look over the contracts and get them back to me as soon as possible." Karen signaled Vita-Jean to hand out the contracts. "Trey Benson came to me yesterday after the service, asking me if we could perform a few of Apollo's songs as tribute for him tomorrow in Miami, and I agreed."

I looked at Antwan, knowing he was about to go off.

236

"Come again?" Antwan made a face.

"We are going on tour tomorrow." Ervin, who sat to A.J's left, spoke up for his wife.

"But—" Brandie, who stood alongside the wall with the other dancers, cleared her throat. She glanced at Antwan. "I thought y'all would postpone the tour for a little while being that Antwan's brother just passed away."

Karen looked at Brandie with 'where they do that at' written all over her face. "We leave for Miami tomorrow," Karen replied.

Antwan stood up from leaning against the wall. "Nah, man. My muthafuckin brother just died, and y'all niggas want me to perform? Hell nah! I ain't performing shit!"

A.J. spoke up, his domineering voice echoing about the room.

"I just lost my son, Wale, so I know how you feel, Antwan."

"And I just lost my muthafuckin' brother, Apollo, who was your muthafuckin' son too, nigga!" Antwan snarled.

"We leave tonight, and that's it, Antwan. Go home, pack your shit." Ervin shook his head at Antwan. "There's always some shit with you. We're not going through this shit tonight. Your brother's gone. I know it's rough, but the show must go on. Antwan, where are you going?" Ervin huffed, talking to Antwan's back as he headed back towards the door to the conference room.

"Yeah, it can go on, without me, muthafucka." Antwan held his middle finger to the sky as he left out the door.

***

I couldn't let Antwan ruin his opportunities and the ones of his friends who depended on him. No one could find Antwan that night. Karen had booked everyone's reservation, including mine, at the Biltmore Hotel. Once I found out that Antwan canceled his reservation, I cancelled mine as well. I wasn't going without him, despite the fact that Sean was staying behind with A.J. Miller to catch a later flight that night than the rest of us. Karen wanted me on the first flight to ensure that I was on time when they had a meet and greet that night at a club in Miami. I was in no mood to meet anyone let alone go on tour in the first place.

Antwan's friends looked everywhere for him that night. Our flight was leaving at 9:15, and it was 7:30. I knew just where Antwan was.

"What are you doing here?" Antwan asked, seeing me strolling up to meet him on the rooftop of his apartment building in Bethesda.

"You didn't think I was going to Miami without you, did you?" I asked, sitting down next to him, alongside the pool.

Antwan's temples twitched. "Don't miss your opportunity, shawty."

I scoffed. "Don't miss yours."

Antwan just looked at me.

"Your friends are depending on you, Antwan. The same friends that you brought from the streets with you into fame are looking up to you. You know Queen didn't want to do this; she's doing this for your, boo. You can't let them down." I looked his handsome, sad face over.

"I just wanna give up, Lyric." Antwan shook his head at me.

"You can't quit. Apollo wouldn't want you to quit." I tried to convince him.

Antwan scoffed. "The fuck you know about what Apollo wouldn't want me to do? He wanted me to stay rapping underground and not take my shit to any of these fucked up ass labels, but I wouldn't listen. He knew it was all bullshit. I just found out that Sean is gonna be A.J's partner, that this nigga is about to basically own my ass. I thought he was just working for A.J., but his bitch-ass mama was right—the nigga is gonna own every right to everything that I've ever sung underneath Instinctive."

I nodded. "I know. If I marry him, I'll take part ownership in your music. I'll have access to royalties for your songs. He can't reproduce or sell your songs without my permission since I'll own your songs, too."

Antwan's facial expression softened a little as he looked my face over. "You—" He wasn't quite sure what to say. "You're marrying this nigga so—so that I won't lose it all, huh?"

I hesitated. "Maybe."

"Why are you doing this for me, Lyric?" Antwan asked. "Why did you stay behind and wait for me to make it out of that club? Why did you stay with me at the hospital? Why did you have to know the lyrics to my mother's songs in that book that nobody knows about? Why do you care so much?"

"Everybody needs someone, Antwan." I didn't know what else to tell him.

Antwan shook his head. "You don't belong to me regardless. Don't ruin your life with this nigga to save mine, shawty. It ain't that deep. You and I can write more music together. Get away from this nigga before it's too late."

"How long have you been rapping? What, since you were like fifteen? You've made a lot of hit records, hun." I watched the 'fuck it' expression on Antwan's face. I sighed. "I can't let you lose it all just because you wanna be puffed up with pride."

"Why do you even care?" Antwan shook his head at me.

"Shit, why don't you care? You can't give it all to A.J. Miller when you said he was responsible for Apollo's death!" I shoved

Antwan. "What made you wanna rap? Think about whatever it was that drove you to do this before you think about throwing it all away."

Antwan looked at me, shrugging. "I mean, it's the only way I could get out the way that I feel inside without actually acting it out. My mama was the Mayor of Baltimore, and no one knew that shit until she died. When I met her at that group home and I found out that she was my mom, I kept that shit to myself. I didn't even wanna talk about it. Being abandoned just drove me harder to get out the ghetto. I grew up in the hood, being raised by my uncle, who used to beat the shit out of us every day. I just saw my brother get killed just because he had no issues killing any muthafucka who crossed him! Me and my brother weren't supposed to be in the hood when we had two parents who were rich, shit. My brother didn't have to die the way he did. I'm angry, got damn it! I went through hell getting into this got-damn industry. I had to do shit you wouldn't believe to make it as far as I have! I ain't got nothing to sing about. All these muthafuckas wanna do is change who I am. Want a nigga to sing ballads and shit. You can keep that let-me-sing-a-love-song-to-you shit. I ain't no soft-ass nigga. I'm not gonna let these niggas chance my image. My fans love me the way I am. I don't need a broader audience. Once I break away from Instinctive, I'm doing me—gangsta-rappin' to the day I die, Lyric."

"Well, by the looks of the way you're life is going, it seems like death is knocking right at your front door." I sighed.

"Well, then, let it come; I'm ready." Antwan shot back.

"I just met you, Antwan. I wanna keep you around for a little while," I admitted.

Antwan still wasn't backing down. "People in hell want A.C. and ice water. What's your point?"

I rolled my eyes. "Would you stop being so fuckin' difficult? I'm trying to save you!"

Antwan laughed out loud. "Save me? You can't even save yourself! This nigga's got you trapped."

"I chose to take this ring, Antwan. Sean didn't force it on my finger." I tried to tell myself.

"Yeah, he kind of did when he announced the shit live on the radio before he even told you to your face." Antwan had to remind me.

"Look, I can handle my own problems, okay?" I watched Antwan smirking.

"Yeah, I see." Antwan grinned a little. "Good job, Mrs. Lee."

"And we're not talking about me; we're talking about you. You can't give this up, Antwan. You worked too hard." I let him know.

"The fuck do you care? You gonna let Sean run your life. Looks to me like death is knocking at your muthafuckin' door, too. Therapy my ass. How long you think that rehab shit is gonna last? One month? Two?" Antwan watched me stand from my seat.

"Are you coming or what, Antwan? I've never been to Miami." I told him. "We were supposed to go to Miami Beach the week my brother died. After he died, I never went back. I know you're hurting, but please just do this one thing for me, and I swear I won't ask you to do anything else."

Antwan stood from the chair, looking down into my face. He took a deep breath. "What time does the flight leave?

***

We all arrived in Miami that night around 11:00. Since I had canceled my hotel reservation, I had to book my reservation at another hotel. Mariah was coming in on a later flight with the rest of the dance team. I flew in with Antwan and his crew on his private jet, since Antwan had canceled the flight that Karen booked him. The crew was staying at the Biltmore, and I had Antwan's bodyguards get me to the Marriott so that I could get a room far away from anyone else. I had no idea where Antwan was staying, and I didn't want to. I didn't have time for Sean's speculating ass. It was bad enough I couldn't be in the man's presence without Sean trippin'. He wasn't as irrational as he might have been on the cocktail of drugs that he'd been on the day he came back from being on tour with Antwan's crew. But he still smoked weed laced with some sort of drug, just to take the edge off of weaning off of whatever drugs he had in his system. Rehab was just a few weeks away, and it was apparent Sean wasn't going to get off of drugs on his own. I had to keep my distance from Antwan to keep that boy from flying off the handle.

I was glad that I canceled my reservation at the Biltmore. I didn't want to stay in the hotel with the rest of the team, knowing some shit was going to pop up in the company. Tensions were brewing. Antwan was pissed. He knew his father was the reason why Apollo was dead; at the same time, Antwan knew Apollo should have thought before he killed his brother over a girl who didn't give a fuck about him.

"Booked?" I exclaimed at the front desk of the Marriott hotel.

"How the fuck are you booked?"

The front desk agent, Nancy, shrugged. "Sorry, ma'am, we're booked because of the new club opening just a few blocks from here. Not to mention, Antwan Jared is in town and will be appearing at the club."

I was so frustrated. "Well, tell me the nearest hotel to this one please. I am supposed to be at that club in thirty minutes!"

I saw Nancy's eyes widen as she looked over my shoulder before looking back at me.

"She can stay with me." I heard Antwan's voice behind me.

I shook my head frantically as Antwan approached my side. "No, Nancy—no!"

"What's up, Nancy?" Antwan grinned at Nancy. "Yeah, two room keys, please. Shawty's staying with me. Have someone carry her luggage to our room, a'ight?" He winked his eye at Nancy before taking the room keys from her and grabbing me by the hand.

"You've got some nerve, Antwan. Why do you have to be so fuckin' bold?" I asked Antwan, watching him open the door to the hotel room.

"Thank you." Antwan tipped the bellhop as he placed our bags inside of the room. Antwan eyed me as the bellhop left the room, closing the door behind him.

"You know we shouldn't be staying in a room together, Antwan! How does this shit look?" I exclaimed.

"Nobody knows we're staying here together. I paid the front desk attendant enough for her to reserve the room in 'Billy Sunday's' name." Antwan grinned.

I made a face. "Who is that?"

"Exactly." Antwan replied.

I rolled my eyes. "Someone is going to see us. When Sean gets here, I'm pretty much screwed."

"Lyric, you're the only thing keeping a nigga calm right now. You have no idea the thoughts running through my mind. Can I just—" Antwan didn't want to sound like he was begging. "Can I just have my calm until the storm hits?"

I wasn't sure how to respond to that, so I didn't. "I need to get dressed and get to this meet and greet. Are you coming?" I watched Antwan shaking his head, taking off his jacket. "Why? Come on. Don't make me go by myself. Mariah's flight hasn't made it yet. I really don't feel like being there with Karen. I feel like she's trying to sell me whenever I'm around her."

Antwan laughed, walking past me. "Yeah, she'll put a price tag on your ass and sell you to the highest bidder if you let her. She's always looking to make a profit off of someone. My publicist, agent, and a few record executives from Beat the Block are going to be at that club. Not to mention, By Any Means is going to be in the spot, too. They're both trying to steal a nigga from Instinctive. Everyone wants your music, shawty. They didn't know it was your music until Sean admitted that you wrote the songs that he claimed that he wrote for me. All these years, it's been you." Antwan shook his head, taking off the blue baseball cap that Apollo was wearing the day that he died. Antwan went by the club the day after the shootout to help clean up and found the hat on the floor.

THE LYRICS TO HIS SONG

I ended up going to the meet and greet alone that night. The weather was horrible. Sean sent a text, saying that there was a storm in Maryland that was going to delay his flight until early the next morning. Mariah and the dancer's flight was delayed as well. I was alone. I didn't feel right going back to the room with Antwan, even though every inch of my body wanted to. I sat by myself at Club Venture, listening to Antwan and his brother's songs playing over the speakers. The club was filled with record executives and club owners. The club was opening to the public the next day at nine o'clock. Antwan was going to perform in front of about twelve hundred people, and I knew his head wasn't really in it. The songs that he recorded with Apollo were ruthless as a muthafucka, telling tales of what they got into while living in the hood. The twins showed no mercy to their enemies. If there was any truth to the lyrics that Antwan and Apollo sung, they had done things to keep muthafuckas after them for years to come. Killing McKaylah and Wale was the least of the crimes that was committed. Karen wanted to soften Antwan's music to take attention away from the album that Antwan recorded with his brother. She wanted to show a different side of Antwan. She wanted to show that Antwan Jared was more than a thug. That he had a heart.

I didn't stay at the meet and greet very long. Around two o'clock, I went back to the hotel room to find Antwan sitting in a chair facing the window, watching the rain splattering against the glass. Beats By Dre earphones covered his ears. Tears slid down his face. I walked over to him, sitting in a chair alongside his. His hand gripped the arm of the chair as if he was holding onto the chair to keep him from getting up and leaving that hotel to do something crazy. His nostrils were flaring, and his eyebrows were tightly knitted together. I placed my hand on his. Antwan's facial expression softened a little as he loosened his grip on the chair to grab ahold of my hand.

There was only one king-sized bed in the room. I refused to let Antwan sleep in a got-damn chair when it was his room. So, we both decided to sleep on opposite ends of the bed. At least, that was how it started out. I hardly got any sleep that night. I had nightmare after nightmare of Denise giving birth to the twins. Apollo didn't make a sound his first few minutes of life. Denise gave birth to both boys, no C-section, no drugs. She was already in labor when she was rushed to the hospital. She was young, probably about seventeen years old. She was wearing a private school outfit in my dream, so I assumed she was in high school. When she pushed Antwan out, the doctors immediately took him. When she pushed Apollo out, they took minutes to revive him before taking him to the NICU. A dark figure stood in the room the night of her delivery, telling Denise, "This is for the best." I must've had the same dream at least ten times that night. I felt each and every twinge of pain that Denise felt while giving birth to those boys. I woke up screaming halfway through each dream. Antwan crawled his way to my end of the bed, holding me, soothing me through each dream. He didn't know what I was dreaming about, but he knew that I needed him.

I took a nice long shower that morning to drown out the thoughts of the twins' mother. I got out of the shower, stepping out onto the carpet that was spread out in front of the bathtub. I had no idea of what I was going to wear. I used to get dolled up everyday; you would never catch me in sneakers, a t-shirt, or sweats. But Sean's jealousy had gotten out of control. I didn't have time to hear that nigga asking me where the fuck I was going if I had on something that was too tight or too short or wasn't being worn around him. I was lucky he let me rock crop tops or skinny jeans. All I had in my luggage were jeans, tank tops, and capris. I was going to have to wear one of Mariah's outfits because there was no way I was going to wear anything in my sister's suitcase. Mariah's flight came in that morning at around 10:30. She wanted me to go with her to rehearsal. Like I said before, I wasn't a part of this performance. I was just on the road with Antwan, so I could write music, and we could rehearse the songs. Karen had studio connections in every major city, so recording the songs between performances wasn't going to be a problem.

I stood in the mirror, adjusting my bra, when Antwan came into the bathroom, walking past me and over to the toilet like I wasn't standing there. I scoffed. "Really, Antwan?"

Antwan made a "you know you've seen a dick before" face at me before standing over the toilet, which was right next to the sink that I was standing in front of. And he just whipped it out in front of me. I couldn't help but glance at it after seeing something shiny flickering from the corner of my eye. He wasn't hard, but the dick had to be about six inches in girth, maybe about eight inches long. And when he wiped that monster out of his sweatpants, I saw three steel barbells climbing down his dick, at least an inch between the three of them.

I gasped, looking back into his face.

Antwan grinned, looking down at his dick as he peed. "Frenum Ladder—that's what it's called."

I shook my head at him. "What the fuck made you wanna get some shit like that, Antwan?" I grabbed my tank top, throwing it on.

"This crazy ass white girl I used to fuck with had all sorts of body piercing. She told me it would be fun, so I went with shawty to get it done. It wasn't so bad. So I got another one. And then another one. You're lookin' at a nigga like I'm crazy, but the ladies love to climb this ladder. I'm telling you." Antwan watched me roll my eyes as he shook his dick before sticking it back through his boxers.

"Oh, please," I muttered, though I was sure they did. I looked at Antwan as I grabbed my shorts from the countertop and slid into them. He didn't look dressed to go rehearsal. He was dressed in black sweats and a wife beater. "Umm, Antwan, are you going with me to rehearsal? I mean, we'd have to leave at different times, so they won't suspect anything, but are you—"

Antwan cut me off, standing alongside the sink, eyeing his handsome reflection in the mirror as he washed his hands. "What the fuck is the point of going to rehearsal when I'm not going to perform, Lyric? I can't even think of performing. All I have on my mind is revenge, and all Karen is thinking about is money. Fuck her. Fuck that performance. I'm not doing the shit."

And he didn't. Club Venture was packed that night, beyond capacity. The owners were prepared for at least twelve hundred people to show up, but instead, almost two thousand people crowded around the club that night to get in to see Antwan. The cops surrounded the club within a three-mile diameter. The stage was set. The dancers were in place. Mariah was nervous but was looking cute as ever. They practiced for five hours straight that day. And Antwan was difficult through the entire rehearsal.

Our first appearance was at the opening of that nightclub. Everyone was in town to see Antwan perform, but his heart wasn't in it. The crowd was hype, cheering him on without him saying one word. His very presence was captivating. There he was, dressed like he was about to go play ball—wife beater, gray sweats, gray Jordan's, black baseball cap—and you would've thought by the way the women screamed over him that he was dressed in Alexander Wang. Antwan

251

told me that he wasn't going to perform that day, but I didn't actually believe him. It wasn't that he was being stubborn or that he was being defiant, he actually couldn't perform. When the beat to Apollo's The Right One dropped, Antwan broke down. He sat on the stool in the middle of the stage and didn't say a thing. He lowered his head, tears sliding down his face.

"Oh my God." Sheena stood to my left.

I sighed, Queen standing to my right, watching Antwan breaking down from backstage.   No one knew what to do. The crowd gave Apollo a moment of silence and watched as Antwan shed tears for his dead brother.

"Awe, look at my lil cuz." Queen Gates choked back tears, placing her hand over her heart.

"What the fuck is going on?" I heard Karen's voice over my shoulder as she came up behind us.

I sighed, rolling my eyes, pointing out to the audience. "This is what's going on, Karen. You got the boy performing his brother's song when his brother just died a week ago. The crowd knows he needs time; it's sad someone who's known him since he was a young teenager doesn't realize what he needs." I glared at Karen before looking back at Antwan.

The music filled the air around us. We should have felt excitement, but all we felt was pain.

"We love you, Antwan!" Fans screamed.

"Rest in peace, Apollo!" Others chanted, crying with Antwan.

That really broke Antwan down. The crowd was silent, hurting with Antwan. They knew his brother was killed the weekend before. They were a lot more understanding than Karen was. She stood alongside Sheena, arms folded, Prada shoes tapping against the ground.

I had to do something. Oh my goodness, I hated the song that was playing. But I had to help Antwan. They were going to think I was a joke, but I really didn't care. Antwan needed me. Sean, who finally showed up late that evening was behind the turntable on stage, serenading the crowd with his signature beats. He watched as I hesitated out on stage towards Antwan, mic in my hand, sexy, long-sleeved, slim fit, denim jean dress hugging my hips, nude Red Bottoms on my feet.

"What are you doing?" Queen tried to grab my arm, but I pushed her away.

I exhaled deeply, placing the microphone to my lips. And I started spitting the first verse of the song. I was late, but I was there. "Let me tell you about this girl named Trina. She said she wanted a freak in the evening like her name was Adina. She said she had a man, but the nigga won't shit. She didn't wanna talk, said all she wanted was the dick!"

The crowd was hype, even though they didn't know who I was and why I was rapping the lyrics to a song clearly written for a man.

"I asked her how did she want it, how did it feel to fuck with a nigga who had a couple mil!" I approached Antwan, taking center stage. "Shawty was ready to fuck right there in her nigga's car; I said, 'hold up shawty, you're about to take it too far. What happens when your nigga rolls up and unloads?' Shawty said fuck it and started taking off her clothes. She pulled up her skirt and said, 'boy, I got a gun. Your girl, Trina, is a rider; you don' found the right one.'"

Antwan looked up at me, tears racing from his eyes, but a grin on his face as the background vocalists to the rear of the stage began singing the hook to his brother's song. Antwan dried his face, standing up from the stool. I patted him in his chest, letting him know that I was there if he needed me, but I was about to leave the stage. He grabbed my arm, pulling me back to him.

Antwan shook his head at me, thinking I was crazy as I held the mic to my lips, rapping the second verse, his verse. "Here comes her nigga, creepin', askin' muthafuckas, 'man, have you seen Apollo?' 'Last time I seen him, he had Trina's mouth wide open, saying hurry up and swallow.' Her man was heated, pistol swinging, went and got his boyz from the block. He had in his mind when he caught me, he would off me, I was gonna get shot."

I got two verses and a hook in before Antwan got the strength to spit fire for his fans. I don't know where all that adrenaline had come from. I would never hear the last of that performance. Karen was pissed, though Apollo's management liked my version of Apollo's song and my dedication to Antwan to help him in his time of need. I couldn't leave him hanging. When I was on that stage, all I saw was Antwan's tears. He needed me. The band and even the dancers were lost without him. My sister didn't even know how to congratulate me after the show. All she could do was invite me to sit with the dancers in VIP after the show. I wasn't up for it. I used all of my energy on Antwan. If I was going to be any good the following day, I had to go back to the room for some rest. Everyone was headed out to the after party, including Sean, who didn't even bother to ask which hotel that I was staying in. He was feeling some type of way about me backing Antwan up on stage, and at that point, I could really care less. Once A.J. Miller showed his face at the club, I left.

Back at the room, I sat on the bed, packing my clothes. We were headed to Houston the next day to perform in concert. Karen was in search for the second songwriter to add to her team. The entire day before the concert was going to be spent at rehearsal and in the studio. Karen's goal was to get Antwan to the BET awards that summer, and she just knew I could get him there. His music was banned from both

BET and MTV. They claimed his music was filled with violence against state officials and women, and that if he wanted to appear on anything affiliated with their television stations, he had to tone his music down a few notches.

I smiled to myself, folding the dress that Mariah gave me, telling me it looked better on me than it did her because of my long slender legs. I couldn't stop thinking of the look on Antwan's face when I rapped his brother's verse. He looked at me as if I'd brought his brother back to life. Truth was, being around Antwan brought something out in me that I never even knew that I had. Courage. Versatility. Life.

The door to the hotel room crept open. I looked up to see Antwan making his way into the room, closing the door behind him.

I grinned at him before zipping up my suitcase.

"Why aren't you getting ready to roll with ya girl, Mariah, shawty? She said she's about to hit the club with Queen before they check out the after party tonight. She was looking for you at the Biltmore when I swung by there to talk to my niggas in the lobby. She asked me if I knew where you were. I said nah, assuming you didn't tell her that you were staying with me." Antwan approached me.

I stood from the bed, shaking my head, rolling my eyes. "Hell nah, I didn't tell her. I didn't tell anyone. You know this isn't appropriate. I appreciate you not freaking out when I had my nightmares last night. They can get pretty intense. They used to freak Sean out pretty bad."

Antwan scoffed. "That's cuz Sean's a weak ass nigga. He doesn't know what it is to have someone's back unless it's his own. I got'cha back, shawty. No need to thank me."

I just looked into his face as he pulled his hat down over his eyes a little further. He was having a hard time telling me something. "You okay?"

Antwan shook his head. "Nah. I'm just thinking about my nieces, man. What am I supposed to tell them when they ask me where their daddy is? I'ma have to raise these girls on my own. McKaylah's racist ass family doesn't want her kids, and McKaylah already had a nigga listed as the next of kin on their hospital records. I'ma have to get my lawyer to help me get full custody of these girls before the state tries to take them from me."

"I'll help you with the girls. I'm sure everyone will help you, boo," I assured him.

Antwan was still on edge. He looked like he needed some air. "Ummm…You wanna play basketball?"

I grinned. "But it's 12:18 in the morning, at night, however you wanna put it."

Antwan shrugged. "So. Go change."

So there I was, in the middle of the night, center of a basketball court in an empty neighborhood park with Antwan Jared. I don't remember the last time that I had so much fun doing something so simple with someone, a guy at that. Antwan needed to let off some steam. Antwan may have drank a little bit, smoked a little bit, but at least he didn't do the shit around me. There I was, looking cute in my tank top—tied in a knot in the back—and little Adidas shorts, hair pulled up in a messy bun. White ankle socks. Black and white Adidas. Antwan was dressed in his tank top and baggy gray gym shorts, black Polo boxers showing. Gray J's on his feet. "The Hood Raised Me" black baseball cap on his head. He was pretty good at playing basketball. I wasn't so bad myself. I played in high school, though my parents wanted me to keep my head in the books, so I never pursued an athletic career. I got my business administration and management degree and didn't go anywhere with it because Sean promised me that he would take care of me and I didn't have to do anything but be pretty and wait on him to come home at night. That dream shriveled as soon as he got his taste of fame. My athletic opportunities passed, and Sean's dreams soared off. All I had left was writing, which I did on my own private time until Antwan made his way over to me that day in Foot Locker, just a week earlier.

"Damn!" Antwan crashed down onto the bench that sat alongside the court. "Why didn't you tell a nigga you had skills like that?" Antwan frowned at me as I sat down next to him, smirking, guzzling down half a bottle of Peach Lipton's Iced Tea. "I thought ya ass was just gonna look cute and try to dribble the ball around me, but nah! How many points did your ass score? Got-damn!"

I laughed out loud, though I was totally out of breath. "Oh, I know I'm gonna pay for this tomorrow! I haven't played ball in some years, hun! Shit, I surprised myself. I didn't know I still had it. No one plays ball with me."

Antwan grinned, drying the sweat from his face with his shirt. "You can play with my balls if you want."

My eyes widened as I shoved him. "Nasty ass."

Antwan laughed a little. Though he was sweating, looking like he just stepped out of the shower, when the wind blew past us, oh my goodness, the smell of his Giorgio Armani cologne flowed through my nose, nearly crossing my eyes. Antwan's smile faded. "Whenever I was on tour, my brother would fly out to meet me. Me and my crew were on tour a lot this year, but I swear, I felt like I never left home. Apollo was always flying out to meet me, and whenever he did, we would get a group of niggas together and play ball. Apollo stayed whippin' my ass on the court. My brother had so many skills but would never use them. It took me years to get him to record in that studio, and the moment BAM record executives heard the first few bars of his song, they were shoving that muthafuckin' contract in his face!" Antwan laughed to himself, before his eyes glossed over.

I turned to him on the bench. "I know it's hard; trust me, boo. I lost my brother, and not a day goes by that I don't miss him. You never get over losing someone who was so close to you. That hole in your heart stays there forever. Nothing fills that void. All you can do is concentrate your energy on something else that you love. You have your music, you have your friends, you have your fans."

Antwan looked at me as he slouched back in his chair. "What about you? Sean doesn't need you, shawty, I do. Let me have you."

I shook my head at him. "That's your grief talking, hun. You and me together? Don't you think that would complicate things just a little? I mean, I am engaged."

Antwan sucked his teeth. "I bet I know more about you than ya nigga does. Ask me one question about you, and watch me get the answer right."

I looked at him, hesitating for a minute. "I'm not doing this with you."

"C'mon, ask me one question, and I bet I know it. C'mon, try me." Antwan's eyes searched my face.

I nodded, grinning a little. "What's my favorite ice cream?"

Antwan shook his head. "You don't have one. You're lactose intolerant. I know because right after you ate that got-damn mac and cheese at Carolina Kitchen, your ass was steady going to the bathroom. You know that shit gave you the bubblies. I don't even know why you even ate that shit!"

I laughed out loud. "It was so good too! Okay, what about my favorite brand of clothing?"

Antwan looked at me, shaking his head. "I need to be calling you Adidas because that's all you rock outside of the cute get-ups you've been rocking to my shows and to that fake-ass engagement lunch at your parents. Man, come on, ask me something hard."

I sighed. "Why did I fall for someone like Sean?"

Antwan looked at me. "Because you were looking for someone like your father. We only go for what we know, shawty. It's sad but true."

I sighed. "I have needed something like this, Antwan. I don't get this kind of attention. Ever. And I need it. Thank you." I had to tell Antwan.

He shook his head, "Why would you thank me? It's not like you're not doing me any favors. I don't know when the last time I went somewhere without bodyguards. I don't remember the last time that I got to just enjoy someone's company without feeling the need to check my phone and see which calls I missed. From the day I met ya ass at Foot Locker, you had a nigga's back. These muthafuckin' shoes go with every got-damn thing." Antwan grinned a little.

I rolled my eyes. "No, seriously, I have to thank you. For giving me this opportunity and for respecting me. I have been meaning to tell you that, outside of barging in the bathroom on me, you have been a perfect gentleman." I grinned at him, patting his shoulder before bending over and picking up the towel that I'd dropped on the ground.

"Yeah, about that," Antwan grinned, eyeing my thighs a little before looking back into my face. "You ummm, you really came through for me today, real talk."

I shook my head, sipping from my bottle. "Nah, boo, I just did what anyone would have done."

Antwan disagreed. "Who else stepped out there the way that you did? You hate that got-damn song!" Antwan laughed to himself, watching me roll my eyes. "But you knew every word, not missing a lick. You say you're scared to step out there on stage, but I can't tell. I was lost out there on that stage without Apollo. I miss him like a muthafucka. I feel like a part of me is gone, and no one knew how I felt except for you. No one else knew what I needed tonight but you did, Lyric... My Lyric. When I can't find the words to say, it's like you always know them. You're the shit, shawty."

My heart thumped in my chest as I lowered the bottle from my lips, watching Antwan grip my thigh in his hand. "You're a good dude, Antwan. I was just doing a good deed for someone who just lost someone that he loved. I wasn't just gonna leave you hanging like that."

"Just when I thought no one understood me, here you come, Lyric. You know just what to do, you know just what to say." Antwan took a deep breath, letting go of my thigh, taking the bottle of tea out of my other hand, sitting it on top of the bench. "Nah, I can't let you marry this nigga. Give the nigga his ring back."

I laughed a little to myself. "What, Antwan? Boy, stop. I had a lot of fun whippin' your ass out here on the court tonight, but it's getting late. If you run, you can catch your boys at that after party. A lot of bad bitches are gonna be in the spot tonight. After seeing your sensitive side, I'm sure a few of them will be waiting and willing to suck the life out of you, literally. They'd love to climb that ladder of yours." I rolled my eyes, getting up from the bench. "What time does the party start? It probably already started." I attempted to walk past him when he hopped up from the bench and grabbed my body to his, his lips pressing against mine. Again.

"The party starts now. Out here in the park. We're alone. No one's watching. I'm sure your nigga knows you're with me. Let's piss ya man off some more. I'm sick of waiting. I think a week is long enough. Don't you?" Antwan whispered between kisses, sliding his hands around first my bare shoulders, then my neck, then through my hair.

I squealed in his mouth, pulling my lips from his, shaking my head frantically. "Ugh-ugh, Antwan, no!"

Antwan was kissing my forehead, then my cheeks, then my ear.

"You know Sean doesn't deserve you. He's never there for you when you need him. The nigga stays fuckin' up on his job; you should've laid the nigga off years ago. As a matter-of-fact, you should have never hired the muthafucka!"

"But you said fuck love, remember?" I sighed as Antwan sat back down on the bench, pulling me down with him onto his lap. I straddled his lap as he wrapped my legs around his waist. His hands slid around my waist, fingers slipping below my waistband. I squealed as his hands cupped my butt cheeks, squeezing them a little. "Antwan, you said you didn't have time for love, remember? Stop it!" I giggled a little.

"Yeah, I know." Antwan exhaled deeply, eyes searching my face. "But I can make time for you. You're more than love, shawty—you're life. And I need you. Nah, I don't wanna fall in love, but I don't want to lose you to that nigga either. Let's just have a little fun, no strings attached, see where it goes, huh? Can we do that? I just met you, but right now, you're the only thing keeping me going. You already know I wanna go fuck up some shit back in Maryland. You're all I have left of my brother or my mother." Antwan kissed my lips. "Don't give my heart to this nigga; he doesn't deserve it. I deserve it. I deserve all of this." Antwan gripped my butt cheeks tighter in his hands. "Got-damn, your ass fits perfectly in my hands."

I shouldn't have been in that man's lap. I shouldn't have been kissing him. Oh, why did I let him slide his hands down my panties? My body shivered up against his as he slid his fingers down the crack of my ass, sliding in between my pussy lips.

"This is wrong." I sighed, as his lips brushed against my neck. "I don't even know you. You don't even know me. We're moving too fast! We need to stop... It's only been a week, Antwan."

"Yeah, but a nigga is already attached to you." Antwan whispered. "Come on; fuck with a nigga. I won't hurt you, Audrey, I promise. We don't even have to put a label on us just as long as there is an us." His lips touched mine again. "Shit." Antwan moaned in my mouth, lifting his butt up from the bench so he could slide his pants down enough to get that pierced dick through the opening in his boxers.

I squealed as Antwan slid the leg of my shorts up just a little, enough to get to my panties so that he could slide them to the side. Everything happened so got-damn fast. I don't even remember if he lifted my body up, or I lifted my own up, or if it was a combination of both. All I knew was I was moaning in his ear as he slid that big, throbbing, pierced dick through me, his piercings sliding against each ripple of my pussy walls. I just knew that I was going to orgasm right then and there. I swear, though what we were doing was wrong, that Frenum Ladder felt like the stairway to Heaven.

Antwan moaned, hands sliding up my torso, left hand cupping my breasts, the other slightly around my neck. "This nigga has to be out of his muthafuckin' mind!" Antwan yelled out before tugging on my ponytail.

This dude had me wide open, about to fuck him on the bench in a park. I had never done anything to that extreme. All of my firsts were with Sean, and there I was, making new memories with Antwan. Every moment with Antwan felt so damn good, but we were wrong.

Afraid to pounce on the dick, I leaned forward, body resting on his, face buried in his neck. "Antwan, we can't do this." I sighed as Antwan's dick throbbed inside of me. I wanted to ride the fuck out of him, but guilt started to set in. "Sean, he—"

Antwan grunted, sliding his hands down to my waist, holding my body against his as he maneuvered our bodies so that he was laying between my legs and we were lying there on that wooden bench, his body pressed against mine. I guess he didn't wanna hear another word about Sean. There I was, kissing Antwan, holding his face in mine as he started to dig into my soul. My heart pounded against his. I squealed with each stroke that he gave, the balls on the ends of his piercing pressing against my slippery walls with every stroke. Though we were fully dressed, the fact that he was inside of me as if we were completely naked sent my hormones soaring. Antwan bit my bottom lip a little, before sucking my lip into his mouth.

"We need to take this back to the room, shawty." Antwan moaned between kisses. "I want to take all of your muthafuckin' clothes off. It's too dark out here; I need to see that pussy. It feels fat as a muthafucka."

I sighed, heart pounding, nodding in agreement, melting in his mouth. "Okay."

My phone vibrated, laying on the bench, above my head.

Antwan reached above my head for the phone. He pulled his lips from mine, looking at the display. He gave me a quick glimpse of Sean's name flashing on the display, and before I could stop him from answering it, he answered it. "What's good, homie? The fuck you want?"

CPSIA information can be obtained
at www.ICGtesting.com
Printed in the USA
LVHW04s1557240718
584775LV00011B/744/P

9 781542 524797